THIRST OF THE RAIN GOD

Secrets of the Maya

J.A. Kalis

Thirst Of The Rain God

Text copyright © 2019 J.A. Owczarczyk

ISBN-10 : 1705522033
ISBN-13 : 978-1705522035

Cover design: twinartdesign

Edited by Emma Clements

This is a work of fiction. All of the characters, organizations and events portrayed in this novel are either products of the author's imagination or are used fictitiously.

For my husband

Other books by J.A. Kalis:

- **When The Jaguar Sleeps**
  A Jungle Adventure
  The Curse Of Inca Gold Book 1

- **Wrath Of The Jaguar Man**
  The Curse Of Inca Gold Book 2

- **The Travel Mate**
  An International Suspense Thriller

CHAPTER 1

The man sitting opposite Travis squirmed in his chair and, with an impatient sigh, scanned the waterfront terrace on which they were seated, and then the adjoining, rather sordid-looking dining area. He had sharp features, and was immaculately clean-shaven; his hair was well cut and neatly combed. He slumped back in his seat, looking annoyed, and Travis saw disappointment dull his eyes.

'I'm tired of waiting. I'm famished,' the man complained, drumming his fingers on the wooden armrests. 'Why is our food taking so long? Does the cook need to catch the chicken and kill it himself?! If I'd known it would take this long, I would've ordered something else.'

'Relax, Randy! Can't you see the place is

packed. Remember, rule number one if you want to survive in this country: You need to be patient.' Travis watched him glance around. But the waiter, a portly man with thick, wavy, black hair and a small, bristly moustache, was nowhere to be seen.

The restaurant was full, all tables taken. Loud chatter filled the air, interspersed with bursts of laughter. To Travis's left, a group of young people – probably foreign backpackers, judging by their appearance and the clothes they wore – were collapsing in helpless giggles while trying to decipher the menu, which was entirely in Spanish. A few tables further along, a family of six talked loudly, competing with one another, raising their voices in an attempt to be heard above the collective din. The tiny town of Flores, located on an island near the southern shore of the *Petén Itzá* lake, was swarming with tourists. No wonder. The impressive ruins of Tikal, one of the most powerful cities of the ancient Maya civilization, were only a short distance away, scattered through the lush *Petén* jungle.

'I'm paying you to take me to the dig site, not to tell me what to do. Is that clear?' Randy fixed him with a heavy-lidded stare, his green eyes alight with challenge.

Those bluntly spoken words hit Travis like a physical punch. His face tensed in response. He straightened up. He wasn't going to put up with this kind of insolence.

'Hey, no need to be so brusque! I'm well aware of what you're paying me for. I just gave you free advice. A small favour. Consider it a bonus. Don't worry, you'll get your money's worth. I know the jungle better than anyone. You're lucky to have found me, but don't push your luck, or I may change my mind. And it won't be easy to find someone else willing to go there. Especially for the price I gave you. You'd need to pay at least twice as much. Like I said earlier, that part of the Guatemalan jungle is very dangerous.' Travis poured some beer from the brown bottle, damp with condensation, into his glass and took a couple of long, slow swallows to calm himself down.

What an arrogant prick, he thought, staring, brows knitted, at his table companion who, seemingly ignoring his outburst, began fiddling with his mobile. There was something about the man he didn't like. Something that irritated him, without knowing exactly what it was. Was it his well-groomed appearance? The overconfidence that emanated from his demeanour? The hawk-like eyes that held him in a steady gaze as he talked? Or maybe it was the air of superiority he exuded?

He had agreed to be his guide and take him to an archaeological dig site buried deep in the jungle because he needed the money. But also because he was unable to resist the lure of a treasure hunt. He knew that the now rainforest-clad Guatemalan lowlands of *El Petén* were once, many centuries ago, densely populated, filled with thriving towns and cities. As a matter of fact, this was the heart of the ancient Maya civilization. So there were probably thousands of complex and intricately carved stone structures and countless stunning artefacts hidden beneath the jungle floor. But it wasn't easy to find them.

The dig site they were going to was located in an area where the once-powerful dynasty of the Snake Kings reigned – a dynasty shrouded in mystery. He was excited to see what the archaeologists had unearthed out there. Vestiges of one of the Snake Kings' lost cities?

Yet he was a proud man who knew his own value. He wasn't going to let this guy treat him as an inferior. Who did the pretentious idiot think he was? His boss? A great reporter? In fact, he looked more like a small-time journalist on the hunt for some sensational piece of news, hoping to get lucky and write a story which would hit the headlines and bring him fame. That was surely why he had come here, to Guatemala. He wanted to be the first to write about the amazing find deep in the jungle. Why would he bother, otherwise? The only problem was, he couldn't go there alone, as that part of the rainforest was one of the most treacherous and dangerous places in the country, due to the fact that various criminal organizations had turned it into their hangout. Over the years it had become the perfect place for ruthless drug traffickers, human smugglers, grave robbers and *contrabandistas* who could operate there in relative obscurity. That was undoubtedly why he needed someone like Travis. Someone who knew his way around the area, knew the dangers and how to avoid them.

Out of the corner of his eye, Travis saw the portly waiter. He was approaching the table occupied by the noisy backpackers, holding a tray of drinks up high. Then, just a step behind him, another server appeared with a couple of big plates in each hand.

A spicy aroma wafted his way, making him realize how hungry he was. Randy was annoying him with his complaints, but he had to admit that their food was taking a long time. They had ordered over half an hour ago. Despite himself, he too started to lose his patience. He raised his hand to attract the waiters' attention but both men ignored him before disappearing behind the swinging kitchen door.

In one gulp, Travis drained his glass and, in search of distraction, looked at the lake stretching away into the distance. From his seat he had a good view of the lake and the surrounding countryside. The sight before him was truly arresting. The day was nearing its end. The setting sun was a huge glowing ball hanging low in the deep amber sky, which was tinged with crimson and garnished with a sprinkling of grey clouds. It crept lower and lower, sending a bright streak of light across the murky, jade-green expanse of water, which gleamed and scintillated as the light danced on its slightly rippled surface. Straight across, on the opposite shore, an almost solid, dark mass of vegetation loomed like a thick defensive wall.

The jungle.

That was where they would head to the next day.

The lush tangle of trees and underbrush stood stark against the burnished orange light, looking uninviting, even ominous. Above the distant treetops, a large bird, probably a heron, soared, its broad wings held out straight.

Suddenly, the air resounded with harsh cries, audible even through the noise of the restaurant. He couldn't tell what creature the cries came from. Despite the warm weather, all of a sudden Travis felt cold. He shivered.

'Listen, Trevor …' His companion's voice jolted him out of his thoughts.

'Travis,' he corrected him.

'Yeah, right … Travis. I guess I owe you an apology.' Randy sank back in his chair and ran a well-manicured hand through his thick, dark brown hair. 'I was a bit too … rough,' he admitted after a slight hesitation, then rubbed his jaw in a weary gesture. 'Must be the exhaustion. Way too many things on my mind lately. Gosh, I've only just realized how tired I am. And I haven't had much rest since I arrived in

Guatemala yesterday. That's why I'm so—' His mobile rang. He grabbed it and looked at the display screen. 'Sorry, I need to take this. It's important.' He stood up, and seemingly feeling obliged to explain, added in a lower voice, 'My ex-wife. My son lives with her.' Then, without waiting for Travis's reaction, he swaggered outside.

When he returned, five minutes later, he looked flushed and agitated.

Just as he slid back into his chair, the portly waiter appeared and set down two large plates filled with rice, black beans and chicken *pepián*, a spicy stew popular in the area.

'Tastes better than it looks,' Randy declared, after chewing through his first mouthful.

Travis didn't say anything to that. Instead, he ripped off a chunk of tortilla, scooped up some of the thick brown sauce and took a bite. The cornbread was soft and warm, the sauce so hot and spicy that it made his tongue tingle.

It's not bad, he decided, and stuffed another piece of it into his mouth.

The group of young backpackers became more raucous. They were talking loudly and gesticulating, every so often erupting in laughter.

They're a jovial bunch, he thought, *or maybe they've just had too much to drink, judging by the number of empty beer bottles on their table.*

Randy cleared half of his plate and took a healthy swig of beer to wash it down. 'I'm glad we don't have to walk the whole way,' he said.

'Yeah, but mind you, we won't be able to go far by car. We'll have to cross a large stretch of the rainforest on foot.' Travis took out a map from his bag and unfurled it on the table. 'Just a moment. Let me see. We can only get as far as here by car.' He jabbed a finger at a spot on the map. 'But there are no proper roads from that point onwards. And, from what you told me earlier, this is more or less where the archaeological dig is. It doesn't look far on the map, but trust me, it's quite a way in such treacherous conditions. And …' He circled an area with his finger … 'this part here is truly dangerous territory.'

'So, it's going to be a hard walk,' Randy concluded.

Travis nodded. 'It's mostly flat, but even so it will be tough. Way harder than your usual stroll in the park. How much experience do you have? Have you ever been in the jungle before?'

'No, never. But I travel a lot. All sorts of places. Both for work and for leisure. I love being active. Keeps me fit. And that's why I'm in rather good shape, as you can see.' A silly grin tugged at the corners of his lips, softening his features somehow. 'Don't worry, I'm used to walking long distances on rough terrain, so I'm not scared of this little trip. I think I can handle whatever comes my way.'

'Nothing compares to trekking through the

8

jungle. Just being in the jungle for the first time can be overwhelming. I don't want to discourage you, but it's better to be prepared. With all the dangers lurking around every corner, you'll need to watch each step you take. Not to mention the awful combination of heat and humidity. It might be pretty wearing for someone who isn't used to it.'

'I guess I can deal with all those inconveniences. I anticipated some difficulties. Don't worry, I'm tougher than I look.' The smile was gone. His eyes darkened, matching his tone.

Travis leaned forward and dropped his voice an octave or two to make sure no one would overhear him. 'Have they found something out there? I don't believe you'd go there just to see the dig. They must have found something worth writing about. What is it?'

Wariness flashed across Randy's face. He chewed another mouthful before he answered, barely above a whisper. 'Yes, you've guessed right. I heard they've stumbled upon something truly amazing. Made a stunning discovery.'

Travis waited for him to elaborate but to his great disappointment, Randy didn't. Instead, he resumed eating his *pepián* in silence.

A few minutes had passed when a commotion to his left caught Travis's attention. He turned his head and saw the group of backpackers leave. He was glad they were going as the noise was starting to get on his nerves.

He hailed the waiter who had come to clear the newly vacated table, and ordered two more beers.

Soon, more people started to leave, and the place quietened down considerably. The men sipped their cool drinks in silence, each lost in his own thoughts.

Travis checked his watch and was surprised to discover it was later than he thought. He drained the last of his beer, set the glass back on the table with a clunk and stood up.

'Time to go back to the hotel. We'd better not stay up too late. We need to leave early tomorrow.'

Randy didn't object. He paid the bill and both men headed for the exit.

Outside, the last vestiges of dusk had given way to velvety darkness. Overhead, the bright moon crawled up the star-speckled, indigo sky, spreading its silver glow. A slight breeze drifted off the lake, ruffling the fronds of a nearby palm tree with a soft rustling sound. It was, however, not strong enough to bring any refreshment. The evening air was warm and damp.

Their footfalls echoing off the cobblestones, they walked down a narrow, dimly lit street.

They had only taken a couple of steps when Travis halted, then retreated into the shadows. His back pressed against a yellow coloured wall, he motioned for his companion to do the same.

'What is it? What's wrong?' Randy enquired,

his voice hushed and nervous. Instead of complying, he took another step forward and Travis was forced to restrain him, gripping his arm.

'They mustn't see us,' he murmured, pointing towards three men who were standing close to a silver car parked at the end of the street. They seemed to be engrossed in conversation and didn't look their way.

The bright pool of light from a nearby streetlamp illuminated the trio. The first two men were rather robust looking. One of them sported a crew cut and was quite short, while the other was taller and had an unruly shock of dark hair. The third man was slender and wiry, had shoulder-length black hair, and a thin moustache adorned his hatchet face. Though from where Travis stood he couldn't see the scar on the man's cheek, he knew it was there. He recognized the man instantly.

It's no coincidence he is here, in Flores, he thought. *He came to get me.*

'Why? Do you know them? Who are they?' Randy's voice was laced with consternation.

'No time to explain it all now.'

'What's going on? They look pretty shifty.'

'Come on. Let's go before they see us,' he urged, inching his way along the wall towards a gap between two buildings. To his relief, it was just large enough for them to squeeze through with ease. On the other side was another narrow alley. A quick glance in both directions told him it was deserted. He stepped into the alley and strode forth without looking back.

'What was that all about? Tell me,' Randy insisted, falling in step alongside him.

'Not now.'

'Why did we have to run away from those guys? Are they looking for you? Are you involved in some shady business?'

'You don't give up easily, do you?'

'I have a right to know.'

'It's not your business. It doesn't concern you.'

'It does. That's the whole problem. Don't you get it? Anything that may jeopardize my plans becomes my business. I hired you to be my guide, not to get me in trouble. What if they follow us into the jungle?'

'They won't. They haven't seen us. So all we should do now is take care to keep it that way,' Travis said more firmly, then added after a short pause, 'Don't worry, I'll get you safely to the dig site.'

'I'm not so sure.'

'You don't need to be. I'll still do it.'

They had reached the small family hotel in which Randy was staying. It was a turquoise-coloured building wedged between two bright orange ones, with a red corrugated iron roof. Travis cast a quick glance around. He relaxed a little, seeing that the men hadn't followed them.

He would wait until Randy was safely inside the hotel, before heading to the flat he was renting a couple of streets away.

'Well, I don't have time to look for another guide,' complained Randy, by way of a farewell. 'So I don't have much choice. I guess I'll have to take the risk – I hope I won't regret it.'

CHAPTER 2

The trail Travis and Randy had been following for about an hour was riddled with tree roots, making it rough and slippery, and in the dim light of the early morning it was hardly visible. It had started out fairly level, but as they progressed it had grown narrower and more twisty until, in some places, it had almost disappeared amid the encroaching undergrowth.

Randy placed each footstep carefully so as not to trip over the gnarly roots and jagged pieces of rock protruding from the ground, at the same time ducking and weaving to avoid the low hanging branches and thorn bushes. Despite his efforts he still managed to snag his clothes and trip over clumsily.

Feeling parched, he paused in the shade of a tall palm tree to take a swig from his water bottle. The initial rush of excitement brought on by his new surroundings hadn't worn off yet. The thrill of adventure still bubbled in his veins. The thought that anything could happen in this vast, inhospitable wilderness exhilarated more than scared him.

The cool liquid instantly revived his senses, and he looked around, eagerly absorbing every inch of the scenery that unfolded before his eyes.

A sea of green leaves stretched in every direction. White gossamer strands of mist rose out of it, swirling lazily and coiling around moss- and vine-covered branches. Here and there dewdrops sparkled where they were touched by the sporadic sunrays penetrating the dense canopy above.

Even though the jungle looked exactly the way he'd expected it to, it still somehow surprised him. When he'd first stepped out of the old pickup truck in which they had travelled for about an hour and a half, the lush tropical forest surrounding them on all sides seemed to be an impenetrable, almost solid mass of tangled vegetation. But gradually, as they'd advanced into it, the thicket had begun to take shape, and soon he was able to distinguish individual trees and bushes in it. Not that it helped much. The immense diversity of plants was dazzling. He had never expected to see so many different types of undergrowth. He'd only succeeded in identifying a few of the species, as the majority he had never seen before.

And then there was the incessant noise. He was unprepared for it and found it quite unnerving. The air reverberated with the pervasive drone of cicadas, interspersed with the clicking sound of long toucan bills, the shrieking of parrots and the haunting cries of howler monkeys.

The jungle trek proved tougher than he had anticipated. Although they'd only just set off, the merciless combination of heat and humidity was already starting to take its toll, and it was affecting him more than he cared to admit. His body had to work harder than usual to keep moving at a normal pace. The moist, stifling air was heavy with the earthy smell of rotting leaves, making it difficult to breath. His sweat-soaked clothes clung to his skin and damp tendrils of hair stuck to his forehead and neck. The deeper they went, the worse it got. He was already barely coping with the adverse conditions, and feared it wouldn't be long before the weariness set in and he'd be forced to take a lengthy break to restore his lost energy.

He wiped his forehead with his shirt sleeve, ran a hand through his hair to smooth it down and undid a button on his shirt, hoping to get some relief from the stifling heat.

'Tired so soon? Come on, we've just started.

Don't get too far behind. It's dangerous, you might get lost.' Travis stopped a few metres ahead. Unlike Randy he seemed oblivious to the brutal conditions and the harshness of the terrain, maintaining a brisk pace despite the well-stuffed rucksack strapped to his back. Not that Randy considered it such an exceptional performance, as the man was probably a couple of years younger than himself and more sturdily built. Besides, unlike him, he was used to walking in the jungle.

With a couple of long strides, Randy closed the distance between them, trying to prove that he wasn't struggling. They continued on at a faster pace and advanced into the thicket. Their bodies reeked with perspiration, and myriads of flies and mosquitoes swarmed around them, buzzing with an annoying insistence.

More and more daylight filtered in through the canopy above, chasing away the last of the mist. All around them new shades of green appeared, more vivid and saturated. Here and there, the bright sunlight streamed in slanted shafts through gaps in the foliage, mingling with the dappled shadows on the forest floor, giving the jungle an almost ethereal appearance.

Staying a step or two behind, Randy kept shooting furtive glances at this man whom he'd hired as his guide, unsure what to think of him. The incident of the evening before had ignited an ember of distrust in his mind. He couldn't shake off the sense of unease that had begun to creep over him. The more he thought about it, the more doubt assailed him. He wondered whether he had made the right decision, risking travelling through the jungle with someone like Travis. But it was too late to turn back now.

The silence between them stretched until it began to weigh on him.

'There must be a lot of wild animals living in this jungle. Won't they attack us?' Randy asked, trying to strike up a conversation.

'Wild animals don't frighten me. They shouldn't bother us if we don't bother them. I'm more worried about some of the humans we may encounter.'

'What about jaguars though? I have no wish to become prey to one of those.'

'The chance of meeting one is very low, as there are very few of them left living in the wild. And anyway, they mostly hunt at dawn or dusk.'

A few more minutes passed before Randy continued with his enquiries.

'Why did you run away from those men yesterday in Flores? Why were you so afraid of them? Who were they?'

'I didn't run away. I just didn't want to cross paths with them.'

'So you say! Why?'

'They looked dangerous.'

'Give me a break. I got the distinct impression you've met them before.'

'You got the wrong impression. I haven't.'

Randy wasn't someone who got easily fooled. He didn't believe Travis. His vague and curt replies only triggered Randy's curiosity and deepened his distrust towards him. It seemed like the guide had something to hide, making him wonder what dark secrets he kept. Eager to learn a bit more about the man, he decided to continue probing, however this time he approached him from a different angle.

'Where do you come from originally?' He slapped at a mosquito that was humming around his ears with an irritating persistence.

'I'm American.'

'I know that, but tell me then what a guy like you is doing here, in this country?' He did his best to sound casual and uninterested.

'I work as a jungle tour guide.'

'You know perfectly well that's not what I mean. What brought you to Guatemala? Have you been here for long?'

'I see why you chose to become a reporter. Can't stop asking probing questions, can you? Talking while walking will tire you out – better keep quiet and enjoy the scenery. Get a good look at the raw beauty that surrounds you.'

What an arrogant jerk, Randy thought. *How dare he patronize me? He seems to have forgotten that it's me who hired him. It's me who's paying his salary.*

'I get it, you've decided not to play the friendly type anymore. Okay, that's fine with me. As long as you get me to the dig site, I don't care.'

'Listen, I don't like anyone prying into my personal life. So don't, okay?' Travis raised his voice as he turned to face him. A bright spot of colour appeared on both his cheekbones.

'Okay, okay, no need to get so excited. I wasn't prying, just making small talk to help pass the time. I just wondered how you happen to know the Guatemalan jungle so well. I bet there aren't many Americans who do.' He tried to sound as calm as he could.

I'd better tread carefully, he decided. *He's clearly touchy, and easily offended. I could tell that yesterday in the restaurant. The thing is I need him here, in the jungle. So I'd better be careful and try to avoid antagonizing him. Gosh, I hope it won't take too long to get to the dig site.*

He thought he detected a slight embarrassment in the way Travis rubbed the stubble on his chin and pushed a few loose strands of shaggy, dark blond hair away from his face.

'Sorry, I guess I overreacted,' Travis's voice sounded softer than before. 'It's just that I'm not used to small talk. But if you must know, I have been living here for close to two years. Before coming to Guatemala I travelled around, visited many different countries. Guess I caught the adventure bug. How did I get to know the jungle so well? I have a friend who is a guide. He showed me around.'

It's not much, but it's a start, Randy thought, supressing a smile.

'You're not married?' he queried further, injecting warmth into his voice, hoping to sound even more approachable and engaging.

'No.'

'Haven't met the right woman?'

'You could say that. As a matter of fact I have never had time to date women. Never had what you might call a serious relationship.'

'I was married once. Mind you, not for long. It lasted barely four years and ended in a divorce. The thing is I have to work long hours, travel a lot. My wife couldn't cope with it. She had enough of my being away most of the time. So she left me.' He wasn't going to tell Travis the truth, which was that she'd found out he had cheated on her. Twice. After a short hesitation, he added, 'I've got a son. He's eleven. Lives with his mother but comes to stay with me from time to time. I'm not happy with the arrangement. We don't see each other often enough. I wish we could spend more time together.'

Randy went quiet, fiddling with the straps of his backpack. The thought of his son saddened him. That last part was true. He wished he were less busy, could spare more time for his only child. The problem was he couldn't, not without jeopardizing his career. And it was a risk he wasn't willing to take.

Travis kept quiet and continued marching on, proving to Randy that his new, more friendly tactic wasn't working either.

After about two hundred metres, the path cleared.

'How strange. This part of the path looks rather well-trodden,' Randy remarked, arching his brow. 'How come? There aren't any people living here, are there?' He was quite relieved that the path would be easier to walk along from now on.

Travis stopped and turned to Randy. With measured movements, he unstrapped his backpack and set it on the ground.

'There are a few,' he said. 'Very poor indigenous people who live off the forest. If we continued down this path we would come upon a couple of dwellings they inhabit.'

'What do you mean "*if* we continued down this path". But we *will* continue down this path, won't we? What choice do we have? Where else can we go? I can't see any other paths.'

Travis unzipped the rucksack and pulled out a bottle of water. He took a long gulp. Then, wiping his mouth with the back of his hand, he said, 'The easy part of our hike is over. I hope you're ready for a long, hard slog? It will be much harder than your usual stroll in the park, but you'll get a chance to taste true wilderness. Look here. That's where we're heading.' He pointed at a wild, tangled mass of vegetation to his left. 'See? There are no trails there. We'll have to clear a path, using this.' Seemingly from nowhere, a machete appeared in his hand.

Randy stared at the gleaming metal blade with

awe. It was the first time in his life he had seen a machete.

'And there is one more thing,' Travis continued. 'We're about to enter the dangerous territory I told you about. All sorts of illicit traffickers are active there. Some of them smuggle illegal goods, others humans. There are also those who rob ancient graves of precious artefacts. It often happens in this country that the drug gangs set fire to the forest to build clandestine airstrips for their small planes or to grow opium and marijuana. There are plenty such places scattered throughout the jungle. I know only where a few of them are located. We must avoid stumbling upon any of them if we don't want to end up dead. So from now on we'll have to move with extra caution. Remember, don't ever let your guard down. Keep an eye out for anything suspicious at all times.'

'Have you ever crossed this part of the jungle before?'

'To be honest, I have never ventured that far north into the *Petén* region. I've never been in the zone we have to cross now.'

'Nice, I'm with a guide who doesn't even know the area we are about to enter,' muttered Randy. Then, allowing a note of genuine concern to creep into his voice, he asked, 'And this machete is the only weapon we have?'

Travis didn't reply. Instead, he rummaged in his backpack and pulled out two guns. He handed one of them to Randy.

'I guess you'll know how to use it if the need arises?'

'Yeah, you bet I will. No need to worry about that.' He wrapped his fingers around the butt of the small pistol. It fit perfectly in his hand. He was familiar with this type of weapon.

'It's not much, but it's better than nothing. Of course, it won't help much if we come across some heavily armed *banditos*. In that case we won't stand a chance.'

'What about bullets?'

'I've got enough for both of us. Come on now, we'd better get going. We've wasted enough time talking.' Without waiting for Randy's reaction, Travis began to chop his way through the impenetrable-looking thicket stretching ahead of him. With a grunt of dissatisfaction at the brevity of their break, Randy followed, staying two steps behind.

For the next couple of hours they trudged on, every so often stopping to catch their breath, drink some water or eat some food. The further they went, the denser and darker the rainforest became. The temperature had risen to stifling levels. The jungle seemed to press in on them from all sides.

To Randy's relief, the journey was less treacherous than he'd anticipated. Apart from the usual discomforts, they encountered no real dangers. He began to think Travis had exaggerated when he'd cautioned him about the perils in this part of the country. They hadn't come upon any people or places that would hint at any suspicious activity. And as for wild animals, all he had seen so far were a couple of monkeys leaping or dropping spread-eagled from one tree to another, as well as plenty of snakes. Way too many for his liking. Some of them were slithering between gnarly tree roots, others coiled around branches. Luckily, none attacked Randy. To his credit, Travis managed to steer clear of the nasty reptiles, for which Randy was grateful.

'How far are we from the archaeological site now? Will we reach it before nightfall?' Randy asked.

'Only if we hurry up. We won't if we keep moving at such a slow pace. We've got quite a distance to cover yet. And it's rather late. The day will be over soon.'

Randy chose to remain silent. The brutal walk had sapped much of his strength and he wondered how long he would be able to continue marching. But he decided not to let Travis see that he was tired. He would muster whatever energy he had left and carry on walking.

After drinking some water, they resumed pushing their way through the underbrush. Yet the muggy weather was just so difficult to bear. Randy's feet, encased in the heavy hiking boots hurt like hell. He was certain a few blisters must have already developed. He had to try hard not to remain too far behind.

They had barely walked about five hundred metres when all of a sudden Travis halted. His body stiffened, as if in alarm.

'What's wrong? What is it? Have you seen something suspicious?' Randy enquired, startled.

Travis held up a hand to silence him.

'We are not alone. I think I heard someone. We'd better hide,' Travis mouthed and motioned for him to move closer to a crooked, vine covered tree trunk.

Huddled between the trunk and a leafy bush, Randy strained his ears to pick up the slightest sound. Apart from the usual noises, all was quiet. And yet he wasn't convinced they were safe. Someone might be lurking in the bushes, ready to attack them the moment they left their hiding place. Travis must have come to the same conclusion because he, too, didn't change his position.

They stayed motionless and silent, waiting. Tense seconds passed, then minutes. Nothing changed.

'Are you sure it wasn't just your imagination, or some animal foraging around?' Randy whispered, expressing his doubts.

'I'm positive. It definitely sounded like a human being. I heard footsteps.'

Randy wiped the sweat off his forehead with the back of his hand and once more scanned every inch of the adjacent underbrush. There was not a soul in sight. He craned his neck to get a better view. Again, he couldn't detect any movement. There was nothing suspicious to be seen or heard. He exhaled slowly. The tight muscles in his shoulders and neck began to relax.

Somewhere in a distance, a twig snapped. And then another. And another. Leaves rustled. A bird screeched. Silence followed, but not for long. Randy had just enough time to wipe his brow and then a new sound caught his ear, making his pulse race. A feeble sound, like branches being gently pushed aside. He held his breath.

Someone or something *was* moving through the underbrush. Heading towards them.

A man? An animal?

Curiosity overpowered fear. He needed to know who or what it was. Despite Travis's hand gripping his shoulder, advising him to remain motionless, Randy dared to peer out from behind the tree. A hasty scan of the surrounding area offered no clue as to the origin of the noise. Then, just as he was about to retreat back to his hiding place, a branch swayed a couple of metres to his right. Long blades of grass and feathery fronds of ferns stirred. A shadow moved among the undergrowth.

Straining his eyes, Randy made out the figure of a man. He was short and stringy. Two steps behind him followed another man, half a head taller. They were coming towards them, getting closer. Too close.

CHAPTER 3

Two middle-aged and rather gaunt-looking men emerged from the underbrush. Taking cautious steps and gazing around, they approached a huge tree with a straight trunk and then stopped. Travis now had a good view of both prowlers, because they were no more than five metres from where he and Randy were hiding. From the safety of his bushy shelter, he studied them. Both were rather short, had unruly black hair and wore checked shirts and black trousers. One had a red bandana wrapped around his head and the other had a moustache. Their tanned faces were rugged and deeply lined. He couldn't see any weapons, but that didn't mean they didn't have any hidden in the bags they were carrying.

A surge of adrenaline coursed through his body.

Are there just the two of them, or are there more skulking around? he wondered.

He shifted position and cocked his head. His eyes swept over the surrounding thicket, scrutinizing the shadows between trees and bushes. To his relief, he saw no one else.

He retreated deeper into the brush and gestured to Randy to remain well hidden. Unsure of the prowlers' intentions, he pulled out his gun and held it at the ready. Just in case. His eyes stayed fixed on the two intruders. He planned to act at the slightest menace on their part.

'Are these the *banditos* you told me about?' Randy whispered in his ear. 'They don't look very scary to me. We can take them. I hope there are no others lurking in the bushes though. Do you think there are?'

Before Travis had time to answer, the moustachioed man lifted his hand. A glint of metal appeared in it. Travis stiffened, alarmed. He recognized the broad, double-edged blade of a machete. His grip on the gun handle tightened, and his shooting finger lay tense against the trigger. They must have spotted him and Randy. He craned his neck to get a better view of their movements.

But instead of heading their way, the man turned towards the enormous tree, towering above the rest like a giant pillar, and began to attack it. With brisk, sure movements, he was cutting diagonal grooves in the bark, creating a zig-zag pattern. Meanwhile, his companion fastened a bag to the base of the tree. Then, with the aid of what looked like climbing spikes and a flip rope wrapped around his waist, he began to ascend the imposing tree trunk.

Travis's shoulders relaxed. He lowered his gun and muttered, 'Just a couple of *chicleros*.'

'What?'

'*Chicleros*.'

'I've no idea what that means. Are they dangerous?'

Travis shrugged. 'I don't think so, but it's best not to take the risk. We'll wait until they leave. It shouldn't take too long.'

'Okay.'

They remained huddled between the leafy bush and the gnarly tree trunk until the two *chicle* gatherers had finished what they were doing and disappeared into the thicket.

'Keep quiet and stay on your guard,' Travis directed Randy when they finally dared emerge from their hiding place.

Step by wary step, they made their way through the tangle of vegetation. Even though they were headed in a different direction from the one in which the two men had gone, Travis kept glancing around and listening for any signs of movement. For safety's sake, he decided to deviate a little from the original route.

'There may be more *chicleros* in the area. They usually work in groups, roaming the jungle in search of sapodilla trees which produce *chicle*. They might have a camp somewhere close by. I don't want to risk meeting them, they are a pretty rough bunch. They're known to be hostile to outsiders. You never know who they are working for and how they might react. I heard that sometimes, apart from gathering *chicle*, they work for the drug trafficking gangs, guarding marijuana fields and harvesting the crops. It pays better. Often, with collecting *chicle* alone they aren't able to feed their families.'

'Tell me, what is this *chicke* … *chicle* you're talking about and why do those men … what did you call them? *Chicleros?* Why do they collect this stuff? What do they do with it?'

'It's a natural gum. A milky white, rubbery sap will ooze from those cuts you saw them make in the tree bark. That's *chicle*. It's used to make chewing gum. Did you know that the first chewing gum was made by the ancient Maya? They figured out how to collect *chicle* and make it into a gum which they chewed to keep their breath fresh and to quench thirst.' Travis couldn't resist showing off his knowledge.

'No, I didn't.'

'So, you see, you can still learn a few things from me,' Travis said with satisfaction and smiled.

They hadn't advanced more than a few

hundred metres when the forest darkened, as tenebrous clouds descended upon it. Within minutes, heavy raindrops began to pelt the leaves with a steady drumming sound that drowned out most of the other jungle noises. The soil under their feet quickly turned to mud, sticky and slippery. Undeterred at first, Travis sloshed through the thick sludge, with Randy on his tail, their boots leaving deep imprints at each contact. But the path became more treacherous the farther they went, and their progress slowed.

Travis didn't know how much time had elapsed since they had abandoned their hiding place, as he hadn't checked his watch, but it seemed to him like hours had passed. Tiredness swept over him in waves. They had been walking for too many hours without a rest. And now the rain had thwarted his plans and confused his sense of direction. He didn't know whether they were heading the right way anymore. The one thing he was certain of was that they wouldn't make it to the dig site before nightfall.

He fumbled in his backpack for his compass and a torch. As he suspected, they had wandered too far off their route.

'I'm soaked to the skin! And it's so dark I can't see where I'm putting my feet,' he heard Randy complain. 'Why don't we hang the tarp our hammocks are equipped with somewhere and wait under it until the rain stops? There's no need to hurry, I don't mind if we get to the dig site tomorrow morning instead of today. I'll still have enough time left to explore it and fly back home before the end of the week.'

'Why didn't you say that when the rain started? There's no use doing it now, we're both completely sodden already. We'd better carry on. The rain doesn't usually last too long. It should be over soon and then we'll stop for the night.'

Carefully, they kept trudging on through the mud.

'How are you holding up?' Travis asked, turning towards Randy.

Avoiding his gaze, Randy mumbled something Travis couldn't make out. It was plain to see he was struggling to keep up the pace, but was trying hard not to show he was affected by the harsh conditions.

About ten minutes later, the rain stopped as suddenly as it had started. Yet the jungle floor remained mired in gloom. Straining to see in the dim light, Travis walked ahead, hacking at the undergrowth that obstructed his passage. Fog wrapped the thicket in a moist embrace. The muggy air pressed in on him from all sides. With each step, he had to be careful not to lose his footing.

An ear-splitting screech cut the air, making his pulse race. There was a threatening note to it. More furious cries followed, merging into a deafening crescendo, echoing through the forest. He stopped and gazed up in the direction they came from. He saw two brown spider monkeys wrestling while hanging by their tails high up in the canopy. The tussle didn't last long. Soon, the two nimble, lanky creatures fled, probably alarmed by the unexpected appearance of two human beings.

'Bloody hell, what is this place? I don't believe it! It's swarming with snakes,' Randy exclaimed behind him. 'So many different sorts. It's crazy. They're everywhere! I can't stand the sight of these filthy reptiles, they make my skin crawl.'

'Welcome to the Snake Kingdom. Just watch where you're stepping and keep your voice low,' Travis cautioned him. 'It's not surprising there are so many snakes everywhere. Don't you remember? We are walking in the land once ruled by the ancient Maya Snake Kings.'

'You can say that again. They chose the right name.'

'Actually, they chose it for another reason. They simply considered themselves to be as powerful as gods. The ancient Maya worshiped the serpent. The feathered serpent was one of their most important deities.'

They pushed deeper into the thicket.

'What's that?' Randy asked with surprise.

'What's what?'

'*That*. The massive grey thing over there. Is it a building?'

'Where? I can't see anything.'

'Look here.'

A trickle of unease crept down his spine as his gaze followed Randy's pointing finger.

To his right, he could make out an odd, grey shape through the gaps in the foliage. *A rock?* he wondered.

He shrugged. 'I don't know. We must get closer to have a better look.'

He advanced with caution, unsure of what he might find. Randy followed, just a step behind. Travis could hear his rapid and shallow breathing. All around them the mist slithered among trees and bushes in thick cloying tendrils, resembling serpents.

Shoving aside a cluster of dangling vines and long strands of Spanish moss, he neared the grey form. It looked like a huge, oddly shaped mound.

What is it? he thought. *An ancient Maya temple? A burial site? Ruins of some ancient dwelling?* He felt a stab of excitement as he took a few more steps forward. When he found himself close enough to see more detail he paused, giving his eyes enough time to focus in the low light.

A large stone structure loomed in front of him. Old and no doubt man-made, moss and lichen covered much of the smooth surface. He got even closer so that his fingers were able to trace the perfect contours. It was unlike anything he had ever seen before. The construction jutting out of the ground in front of him was a huge, stone statue of a human head, askew and tilted in such a way as to be facing skyward.

'Well, I never! That's amazing!' Randy exclaimed, stopping beside him.

'It sure is.'

The reporter rummaged in his rucksack and pulled out a camera.

'I don't believe it. It's a head. A giant head! I never imagined we'd stumble upon something like this. It will make a nice story. I must take some pictures of it.'

Clutching the camera, Randy studied each detail of the colossal sculpture rising in front of him, moving slowly around it, trying to pick the best angle for a photo.

Travis stayed close, watching the imposing head which seemed to have been carved from a single boulder.

A flicker of sound caught his ear. A hiss. He recognized it right away. A threatening hiss. He spun, eager to identify its source. A fer-de-lance snake was rearing up, its arrow shaped head and upper body forming an 'S', its long slender fangs exposed. It was readying itself to strike at Randy, who seemed to be oblivious to the danger, being preoccupied with the camera.

Without a moment's hesitation, Travis gripped his companion's arm and pulled him aside. Then he hit the reptile with his machete, cutting it clean in half.

'I told you to watch where you were stepping!' Travis stared at the wriggling body parts. 'You were lucky I saw it before it attacked you. But you may not be so lucky next time. This species is extremely venomous. One of the deadliest around here.'

Randy remained silent. For a few seconds he stood as if rooted to the spot. His face turned pallid and his fingers tightened their grip on the camera. He didn't say anything, but it was clear the incident had scared him.

They checked the surrounding area. About three hundred metres further east they discovered another colossal stone head wedged between two ceiba trees, the most sacred tree of the ancient Maya. Contrary to the first one, the second head stood erect. Long and black liana tendrils twisted their way around its base in a corkscrew, some of the stems reaching as far up as the full, sensuous lips and the rather small but broad nose. Two bulbous eyes stared straight ahead as if they kept watch over the jungle. Patches of yellow lichen and green moss stained both the delicately sculpted cheeks and the square chin, giving a deceptive impression of a blush. A bizarre headdress adorned its top. It seemed to be made of several stone snakes coiled around each other.

Randy took a couple of pictures of the rare statue from various angles, then asked, 'One of your Snake Kings?'

'I'd say a Snake Queen. Its features appear more female than male to me, but as to its age … I don't know. I doubt it was made by the ancient Maya. I think it's probably much, much older than the Snake Dynasty. Take a good look at this weathered stone. It looks as if it has withstood many, many centuries of harsh weather. The Olmecs who inhabited these lands long before the Maya showed up were known to build and bury huge stone heads. Who knows? Maybe it was the Olmecs who carved these, or some other people of another, as yet undiscovered, civilization.'

Randy shot him an astonished glance.

'I must say, you amaze me. How do you know all this? Ancient Maya, Olmecs? I see you are more than just a regular jungle guide. Are you by any chance an amateur archaeologist as well?'

Travis didn't reply, and he could see that Randy was thinking about something else anyway.

'These pictures will be worth more than gold,' Randy's eyes gleamed with excitement. He brandished his camera at the stone head. 'What a discovery! I'll write a fantastic piece about it when I get home. And there is yet more to come when we get to the dig site. My career depends on this little trip to the jungle. And it's going well so far. If my luck continues, I have a good chance of getting promoted.'

'You haven't told me yet, what have the archaeologists have discovered there?'

'Don't be so impatient. You'll find out for yourself soon.'

Travis checked his watch. It was late. Much later than he'd thought. Dusk would fall soon.

The fading light would make it impossible to see anything, and it would be too dangerous to continue walking.

'It's not far now. No more than two or three hours of walking, but we won't be able to reach the camp before nightfall. It will be dark in about half an hour. We'd better call it a day and resume our journey in the morning. There is less mud around those stone heads. I saw a couple of trees perfectly spaced and strong enough to hold our hammocks. All we need to do is clear some of the low-hanging branches.'

They set about preparing for the night, hanging up their hammocks which were equipped with protective tarps and mosquito nets. Having changed their clothes, they crept inside and each wrapped themselves in a warm and dry sleeping bag, just before darkness engulfed the rainforest.

CHAPTER 4

Travis wasn't an early riser. Yet the boisterous, guttural calls of howler monkeys proclaiming their territory roused him from his sleep at the crack of dawn, and judging by the clamour outside, half the jungle had been roused as well. He had never heard such a deafening chorus of howls before. There must have been hundreds of those hellish noisemakers living in the area.

His first reaction was to cover his ears and snuggle deeper into the sleeping bag. He lay there for some time, rocking gently, trying to fall back to sleep. It didn't work. Long minutes passed but he was unable to drift back to the dreamland from which he had been so harshly pulled. The booming roars bounced off the trees and returned, amplified, mercilessly assaulting his eardrums.

Randy must be awake already, he thought. *There's no way he could sleep through such a noisy inferno.*

With some effort, he climbed out of his tent hammock. He yawned, stretched, then shambled over to the reporter's hammock, which was suspended between two trees a little further to his left. When he looked inside he could hardly believe his eyes. The guy was sound asleep! He lay huddled in his sleeping bag, a carefree expression on his face.

Abandoning the idea of clambering back into his hammock, Travis decided to seize the opportunity of having some time for himself and explore a bit more the surrounding area. He waited patiently until it was bright enough to see without a torch. Then he plunged into the thicket, which was still shrouded in mist at such an early hour. A slight drizzle permeated the air. Stealthily, he weaved his way through the dense vegetation, ignoring the beads of moisture clinging to his skin and hair like sticky cobwebs.

He came upon a narrow stream and followed it for a while, until the muddy streambed, strewn in places with stones, became too slippery and treacherous to walk along. He was about to leave the creek when some deep prints in the wet soil caught his attention. He crouched down to get a better look. Footprints. There could be no doubt about it. There were several sets of heavy-boot prints, and they appeared to be quite fresh. He wondered who had left them. *Chicleros*? Or someone more dangerous?

His inquisitive nature won over caution and he pursued the trail, crossing the shallow watercourse and venturing deeper into the forest on the other side. The ground became firmer, and here and there jagged rocks stuck out of it. The prints grew fainter and then vanished in the thick vegetation.

Travis wasn't so easily discouraged. He scoured the forest floor until, finally, his persistence was rewarded. As he approached a patch of soil covered with a thick layer of rotten, brown leaves, he saw more footprints, and continued to follow them.

He hadn't gone far when he became aware of the faint scent of woodsmoke drifting through the undergrowth. Thinking he must have imagined it, he paused to sniff the air, his eyes darting around the thicket.

He hadn't.

His nostrils flared as they picked up the aroma of woodsmoke mingled with the ever-present odour of damp soil and decaying plants. And this time he detected something else: the smell of roasting meat. It seemed that whoever the footprints belonged to had set up a campsite close by, and they were preparing a meal. Again, he scanned the surrounding forest, looking for signs of human presence, but to his dismay, the dense foliage obstructed much of his view and he couldn't see far in the dim light.

He decided it was too risky to venture any closer to the camp. Judging by the footprints in the mud, there were at least five people. And they were probably all armed. Whoever they were, it was better not to enter their territory.

The area wasn't safe. They should leave as soon as possible.

With great caution, Travis retraced his steps to his own camp. As he got close he could see Randy standing by one of the hammocks, wide awake and looking rather agitated.

'Where have you been? I've been searching for you everywhere!' he burst out the moment he spotted him. 'I thought you'd left me alone in the jungle.'

Travis raised a hand. 'Hey, calm down! Why would I do that? You still owe me a large chunk of cash, remember. I wouldn't risk losing it, would I? I woke up early and you were sound asleep. I didn't want to disturb you. So I took a walk around the forest to kill some time.' He thought it was best not to mention the footprints he had seen.

Randy looked askance at him, but didn't say anything.

Impatiently, Travis pushed away the hair sticking to his damp forehead. 'It's getting late. We'd better get going.'

The urgency in his voice prompted Randy to

move. They had a quick breakfast, took down their hammocks, and without further delay resumed their journey.

'You were gone for quite a long time. Did you see anything interesting out there?' asked Randy.

'Nothing worth mentioning. I told you, I was just wandering about. I guess I lost track of time.'

'Really?' He seemed unconvinced.

As they advanced, the heat intensified, but was just about bearable. The terrain was rough and irregular, but firmer than the previous day. Travis quickened his pace, determined to reach their destination before the sun had risen too high in the sky. Every now and then, he consulted his compass to make sure they didn't stray off course, which would have been easy in the lush tangle of vegetation that surrounded them on all sides.

He worked his way through the undergrowth, too focused on not losing his footing to make any attempt at conversation. Neither did Randy. So they ploughed their way through the shadowy thicket in silence. When he glanced at his watch, he was surprised to find that an hour had passed since they'd left their campsite. He cast a furtive glance behind his back to see if Randy was following. The reporter was doing better than Travis had anticipated. Despite the increased tempo, he was tagging just two steps behind.

'We don't have far to go now. If we maintain this pace we should be there in another hour,'

Travis said.

'Great.'

Again, they lapsed into silence while they walked. Travis thought about the man with the scar he had seen in Flores and wondered whether he would leave town or wait for him.

A buzzing noise resounded somewhere above, jolting Travis from his thoughts. He stopped in his tracks and listened, trying to identify its source. It didn't sound like the buzzing of insects. It was more like a small plane. The noise grew stronger by the second, as though it was getting closer. Looking skyward, he caught a glimpse of a flashing white light through the gaps in the foliage. But then the noise faded away and the aircraft was gone.

'Probably those illicit traffickers you told me about,' Randy said, following his gaze.

'Yeah. But they couldn't have seen us. The canopy is too thick. Still, I'm glad we don't have far to go now.'

They continued walking until Travis saw what looked like a path meandering through the undergrowth. He paused to look closer. The path was so faint that it was difficult to see whether it had been made by wild animals or humans. Then, off in the distance, a faint gleam of light shone through the bushes.

Are we at the dig site already? Travis wondered. *It must have been closer than I'd anticipated.* He checked his compass again, and his eyebrows knitted together in a puzzled frown. They had strayed off east. He had no idea how this could have happened – when he'd last checked his compass, not long ago, they had been heading in the right direction.

'Why have you stopped?' asked Randy. 'Is something wrong?'

'I can't say yet. Look! Look at that light streaming in.'

Randy's gaze followed Travis's pointing finger.

'A clearing?' he asked.

'Looks like one, doesn't it?'

'At last! We've made it. It must be the archaeological camp.'

Travis shook his head. 'No. It can't be the camp.'

'Why not?'

'The position is wrong.'

'Are you sure?'

'Yeah.'

'So why don't we see what it is instead of speculating?' Not waiting for his reaction, Randy began to climb through the undergrowth in the direction of the clearing.

'Wait! It may be dangerous.'

'I know, that's why I'm trying to make as little noise as possible.'

'No, Randy. We'd better stay away from this place.'

'And what if you're wrong? What if it is the

dig site? I have to check.'

'Why won't you listen? I told you. It's not there!'

Randy made a dismissive gesture and continued moving forward. Travis followed him, advancing with slow, cautious steps. At a distance of about a metre from the clearing's edge, he ducked behind a thick bush, crouching beside Randy. He peered through the cracks in the foliage – ahead of him stretched a long grassy field. It was empty.

'A secret airstrip, isn't it?' said Randy in a hushed voice. 'It's so dangerously close to the dig site.'

Travis pulled a pair of binoculars out of his rucksack, adjusted the focus for a sharper view, and scanned the grassland ahead of them.

'I can see skid marks. Some of them are fresh. It looks like the runway was used quite recently – the aircraft we just saw must have taken off here.'

'Any sign of people in the bushes on the other side?'

'No, no one's there as far as I can see. But it's easy to go unnoticed in this dense vegetation.' He lowered his binoculars. 'It might be risky to hang around here too long. Come on, we've wasted enough time. Let's go.'

Randy didn't object.

About half an hour later, Travis saw more light gleaming through the foliage. He felt a pang of excitement. This time it could only mean one thing: they were nearing their destination.

'Is this what I think it is?' he heard Randy ask, his voice brimming with anticipation. He must have seen the light too. 'Is it the dig site?'

Travis stopped and turned to face Randy. 'Yeah. According to my calculations we should be there any moment now.'

A smile spread across Randy's face, and his eyes gleamed with excitement. 'Yes! We've made it! I can hardly wait to see what they've unearthed here... I guess now I can tell you as we are almost there... from what I've heard, they've made a mind-blowing discovery. A discovery that may change history. They've discovered what looks like a maze of subterranean tunnels and stone temples hidden under the ancient Maya ruins. Can you believe it? It's so big it could even be a secret underground city! They've only explored a small part of it so far, so it's too early to say, but they've already found plenty of artefacts: statues and wall carvings, rare pottery and exquisite pieces of jewellery. The place is a treasure trove. Can you imagine the value of the artefacts they've found? You are a lucky man, Travis. Thanks to me you'll have the chance to see it all. So, be prepared!' He smirked and then added, attempting to sound friendly, 'I must admit, I enjoyed our little walk through the jungle. It wasn't bad. Not bad at all. Far less demanding and less dangerous than I anticipated it to be.'

Travis didn't bother to say anything to that. He was not in the mood to chat. He took a few more strides forward, ignoring the low-hanging branches clutching at his clothes and scratching his face. Suddenly the trees ahead thinned and he stopped, staring in wide-eyed amazement at what looked like big grey and green mounds jutting out of the ground in the distance.

The straps of his backpack were digging into his underarms, so he adjusted them and moved forward. Sunlight poured in through the gaps in the canopy above, lighting large patches on the forest floor, across which gnarled branches cast weird shadows, resembling crooked figures.

He shielded his eyes against the sudden brightness, scanning the surroundings. To his left he noticed a faint path weaving its way through the undergrowth. He followed it, thinking it would probably lead them to the camp. Eager to reach the dig site as soon as possible, he lengthened his stride. Now he was closer, he saw that what he had initially taken for mounds were man-made, pyramid-like structures, probably built from limestone many, many centuries ago.

He approached the first one. A steep stairway led to the top, and it was overgrown with lush grass and moss. Long tendrils of vines crept along its sides, clamping at the weathered stone construction, as if trying to wrap it in a smothering grip. Ferns and small thorny bushes sprouted in places.

He plucked at a few clumps of moss, surprised by its spongy feel and cool wetness.

'How amazing!' exclaimed Randy coming up behind him, making him almost jump. 'Splendid. The weathered, moss-covered stone and the lighting are perfect. What a unique play of light and shadow. So intricate. Wait a moment, I must find the best angle to take a couple of pictures.'

Randy fumbled with his camera. When he was done, they moved further along the path. As Travis passed the second mound, he noticed a large keyhole-shaped opening, wide enough for a stocky man to enter. There were footprints in the wet soil close to it and patches of overturned earth.

'Looks like the mouth of a cave. That must be the entrance to the underground they are exploring... the entrance to the secret Maya city hidden beneath the jungle floor. Wait a moment, I'll check it out.' Before Travis could stop him, Randy walked over to the gaping cavity and poked his head inside, but quickly withdrew it. 'It's too dark to see anything. And too quiet. I don't think they're down there working. They must still be in the camp. Come on, let's find them.'

They continued walking and Travis spotted a tent, tucked between leafy shrubs at the edge of a small clearing. Then, about a metre away from it, three more.

He took a few more steps towards the camp,

then paused, his eyes darting around the open space. Spades, picks and other digging tools lay scattered by one of the ancient stone structures. To his left, he saw what looked like a kitchen area, shaded by a large tarp hung over a ridgeline that was stretched between two palm trees. There were remains of a campfire, the ash still smouldering.

He wiped the gathering beads of sweat off his forehead with his sleeve. A sense of unease began to creep over him. He didn't know what it was, but something didn't feel right.

It was too quiet, too still.

It felt as if the place was abandoned. He listened, hoping to hear something tangible.

Nothing.

Apart from chirping of birds, buzzing of insects and occasional cries of monkeys, the place was silent. There was no sign of movement anywhere.

He walked over to the nearest tent and peered inside. As he suspected, there was no one in it. Sleeping bags, rucksacks and other items lay jumbled on the floor.

'Hey! Where is everybody?' Randy peered into the second tent. His voice was less confident now than it had been a few moments before, and he rambled nervously. 'How strange. The camp is empty. It looks deserted... it's all so quiet. Where's the dig team? Not that I expected a welcome party, but if the area is as dangerous as you say it is, there should be at least one person keeping watch over the camp. So why there is no one? Where have they gone? It didn't seem like anyone was working in the underground – I couldn't see or hear a thing. And those tools strewn around, as if they were abandoned in haste …'

'Maybe they are busy digging somewhere deep in the tunnels,' Travis suggested.

'Even so, I would have heard something, wouldn't I? At least a faint echo. But there was complete silence.'

Travis moved towards the last tent. He pushed the flap aside and looked inside.

'This one is empty too,' he announced, and was about to withdraw his head from the opening when he noticed a dark stain on one of the sleeping bags spread out on the floor. His curiosity aroused, he swung his rucksack off his back and slipped inside to get a better look.

'Found something interesting?' he heard Randy ask behind him.

He stared at the deep scarlet stain. 'Seems like someone got hurt.'

'What makes you say that? What have you found?' Randy crept in beside him. 'Oh! Blood. Looks rather fresh to me. What do you think, an accident while digging?' he asked, anxiety lacing his voice.

'If it was an accident, then it must have been quite a serious one, judging by the amount of blood. And where is the injured person? He can't be working ...'

'Hmm, you've got a point there.' Randy fell silent for a moment, then said, 'Come on, let's go. We must find them. I need someone to show me around. I've got work to do. Visit the underground. Take pictures. Hear the story behind the discovery. And I don't have much time left to do it all. Tomorrow morning we need to set off on our return journey to Flores. I need to be back home by the end of this week.'

Once outside the tent, Randy put the camera around his neck. 'There might not be enough room in those subterranean tunnels to move about with rucksacks on our backs. We'd better leave them here. All we need are the torches.'

Travis shrugged. 'Do as you wish. I'm taking mine with me. I can easily move around with my backpack. It's not heavy. I'll just leave the hammock and the sleeping bag behind.'

Randy picked up his backpack and strapped it on. 'Mine isn't heavy either. I guess your idea is better. Let's go.'

Travis hesitated. 'Wait a moment. We haven't checked everywhere yet. That might not be the only entrance to the underground. What if they're working somewhere else and that's why we can't hear anything? I'll take a look around to make sure we haven't missed anything.'

'I'll go with you.'

He dismissed Randy's offer with a wave of his hand. 'No need. It would be better for you to stay here in case they come back.'

Travis examined the rest of the ancient structures, then returned to the camp.

'Nothing. No other entrance anywhere. Unless it's so well hidden that I failed to notice it. The one we saw earlier must be the right one.'

Walking at a brisk pace, they headed for the keyhole opening in the weathered stone. As they neared it, a tingle of anticipation ran up Travis's spine.

CHAPTER 5

Travis drew a deep breath, and holding his torch in front of him, entered the ancient stone structure. Randy followed right behind, so close that Travis could feel his warm breath on his neck.

As soon as he stepped across the threshold, a dank, earthy smell filled his nostrils. The chilled air brushed his face. He couldn't tell exactly what it was, but something made him feel that he entered another world, another dimension. He blinked, letting his eyes adjust. Then, swinging his torch from side to side, he glanced around and saw he was in a long, low-roofed tunnel, just wide enough for two people to walk side by side.

The light from the torch threw dancing shadows on to the jagged, moss-covered walls as they moved forward. He felt the ground sloping away beneath his feet – they were walking downhill.

Soon the clamour of the jungle faded into silence. The only sounds were their shoes crunching on the small stones and gravel, and their breathing. After about eight metres the tunnel came to an abrupt end and Travis found himself standing at the top of a flight of steep and narrow steps. They were so lost in shadow that he couldn't see the bottom of the steps or where they led. With one hand braced against the cold, rough stone, and the other gripping the torch, he descended, taking care not to slip.

He stumbled as his foot hit solid ground sooner than he'd expected, and as he staggered forward he saw in the flickering light of the torch that they had entered another tunnel, this one only slightly wider than the previous one.

He looked at the walls as he edged his way around a bend. They glinted and twinkled like a thousand stars. When he looked closer, squinting against the brightness, he detected some black crystal particles embedded in the grey rock. They sparkled each time they caught light.

'I had no idea the underground would be so deep.' Randy fell in step beside him. 'Where are they? They should be moving about, digging. We should be able to hear something. Anything. But it's so still. Deathly still. I tell you the place is empty. There's no one but us.'

'Don't be so impatient. We haven't gone far yet. You told me yourself it's a huge network of tunnels.'

The further they went, the stronger the dank smell grew. With every step, the air became more oppressive and difficult to breath, clinging to him like damp cobwebs. Beads of sweat gathered on his forehead. He wiped them with the back of his hand.

The tunnel widened into a roughly rectangular chamber with a curved roof. Fragments of broken pottery littered the dirt floor. A statue of two intertwined serpents with wide open jaws sat in one corner. It was made of a well-polished green stone, probably jade. The insides of the snakes' mouths were bright red, their long fangs dripping with blood.

There were two tunnel openings on the opposite wall.

'Now what? Where should we go?' Travis felt lost.

A flash erupted a few times in rapid succession. Randy was taking pictures of the statue. When he was done, he pointed to one of the openings, beside which a pile of stones was heaped.

'I think we should try this one. It looks like it was used recently. The earth is disturbed and the rocks have been piled up. That's probably where they went.'

'Okay, you might be right. Let's go. We'll see

where it takes us.'

They squeezed through the narrow opening and walked slowly down the vaulted passage, Travis leading the way. He looked around. The walls were painted red and covered from floor to ceiling with ornate carvings. He paused to examine the chiselled shapes cut so intricately into the stone. Some of them depicted various human figures, both male and female, all wearing elaborate headdresses, ear ornaments and necklaces. Others were of animals: jaguars, snakes, birds and monkeys.

The deeper they ventured into the tunnel, the stranger and less recognizable the carvings became.

'That looks to me like some sort of hieroglyphic writing.' Randy broke the silence, pointing to a pair of neat, vertical columns of odd shapes.

Travis nodded. 'Yeah, that's exactly what I was thinking.'

'Strange forms. I have no idea what they mean. I must remember to ask the archaeologists if they've managed to decipher these inscriptions. I could cite them in my article.' He brandished his camera. 'Can you shine your torch here? The flash might not be enough to get a clear shot.'

When Randy had taken his photos, they continued down the tunnel, which twisted and turned like the body of a giant snake, so that after a while Travis could no longer tell which direction they were heading.

Suddenly, he detected a hint of fresh air. Curious to know where it was coming from, he quickened his pace. A few minutes later he emerged into a huge dome-shaped cavern, arching high above his head. At the centre of it was a cenote, a large pool of crystal-clear, blue-turquoise water. Shafts of sunlight streamed through a circular opening in the roof and danced on its surface, giving it a mesmerizing, silver sheen. Around it were man-made, narrow limestone platforms and plaster terraces, gleaming with moisture and overgrown with moss. Weirdly shaped stalagmites clustered at the far end of the chamber, and above them stalactites hung from the ceiling like the fangs of some ancient monster. In places, the rock formations joined together, forming gigantic columns.

Travis squinted against the sudden brightness and shielded his eyes, looking upwards. Tree roots and long tendrils of vines were hanging down over the edges of the hole in the roof, some of them dangling hardly a metre or two above the surface of the water.

Disturbed by the unexpected intruders, several small birds flapped and fluttered around, squawking in panic before flying outside.

Randy took another step forward and, his voice laced with frustration, said, 'Wow, a natural swimming pool. Amazing. But that's not what we came here for. Where is everybody?! I'm really beginning to lose my patience.' He cupped his hands around his mouth and called. 'Hello, is anyone there?'

The only answer was his own words rebounding off the cave walls.

'Shh! Don't shout so loud,' Travis cautioned him.

Randy scrutinized him briefly without saying a word. Then, he crouched at the edge of the pool and dipped his hand into the water, sending ripples across its smooth surface. 'It's so cool and refreshing. I don't know about you but I wouldn't mind taking a dip. It would be great to wash off all the dirt and sweat from the long journey.'

'We should find the archaeological team first.'

'Yeah, I guess you're right. No time for a swim now. We'd better hurry, I have to leave tomorrow morning. I've managed to shoot some great pictures, but they're not enough for a big story.'

Travis straightened up and looked around the chamber, shining his torch into each shadowy corner. He noticed a semi-circular stone construction extending from the wall, with a dark opening at the bottom.

He walked over to it. It was just large enough for a man to crawl through, so he squeezed into it, careful not to slip on the wet limestone and the emerald green moss. Inside, at the far end, rose a statue of a feathered serpent, a weird creature that was part bird, part snake, one of the main deities of the ancient Maya. Beside the statue stood some orange and black ceramic pots. Scattered among them were various bones, two human skulls and what looked like the skull of a dog. They were all yellowed with age. There was also a knife, its long blade made from smoky, translucent black obsidian, a volcanic glass used widely by the Maya, and mounted on a wooden handle. It reflected the torchlight like a mirror.

An involuntary shiver ran through his body. He crawled out.

'This place gives me the creeps.'

'Why? What is it? What's inside?'

'It seems to be some sort of a shrine.'

Randy dropped to a crouch and peered inside, using his torch. 'Could be an offering or a burial spot. But you're right, it is creepy.'

Travis scrambled to his feet, brushing off his clothes. He examined the rest of the cavernous chamber, which was mired in shadow. Slowly, he swept the beam of his torch across the walls on the opposite side of the pool, revealing cracks and crevices slicked with moisture and lush green patches of moss. The light illuminated the dark spaces between the looming brownish red, yellow and white stalagmites.

Much to his surprise, Travis realized that there were sculptures tucked between the lumpy rock formations too. He moved closer to get a better look. When just a step separated him from the edge of the pool, he stopped.

There he stood as if rooted to the spot, staring at the unusual figures emerging from the shadows. Two of them represented coiled snakes with human heads. The third, a jaguar, mouth wide open, fangs exposed as if ready to attack. The fourth was even more striking than the rest. It resembled a human being seated on a double-headed jaguar throne. Its face was just a grinning skull with an elaborate headdress on top. It was wearing a loincloth but the torso was stripped of flesh, ribs showing. Around the creature's neck hung a necklace made of what looked like snake or jaguar fangs and human eyeballs. The whole sculpture was painted black, red and yellow, but the paint had faded in some places to a dirty white. A grey layer of dust covered some areas. As he looked at it, a feeling of unease gripped Travis, and an icy sweat drenched the back of his neck. He felt a weird sense of a malignant, threatening presence, as if some dark force or an evil spirit lurked in the shadows. Instinctively he glanced around, but he couldn't see anything unusual.

'At least someone here looks pleased to see us,' he heard Randy say behind his back.

He turned to face his companion. 'What do you mean? Who are you talking about?'

'That creep over there. Who else? Look, he's smiling.' He was pointing at the sculpture.

'Oh, right. Do you know what that *creep*, as you call him, represents?'

'No idea, but by the look of him it can't be anything good.'

'It's one of the Maya death gods, a lord of the Maya underworld.'

'I've heard about that. The Maya called it *Xibalba*, right? A macabre hidden universe where the souls of their ancestors went after they died.'

'Do you know what *Xibalba* means?'

'No.'

'It means a "place of fear", because the ancient Maya believed that everyone who entered it would be subjected to horrific trials.'

A grin spread across Randy's face. 'Sounds scary.'

'But there was a way to avoid the underworld atrocities,' Travis continued, ignoring his remark.

'Really? How?'

'To die a violent death. Because then you went directly to one of the thirteen heavens. Only people who died from natural causes went to the underworld. And I think …' He paused for effect. '… we might be standing in front of a gateway to *Xibalba*.'

'Why? What makes you say that? Those creepy figures?'

'Not just that. This pool of water is a cenote, a natural sinkhole.'

'So?'

'The ancient Maya regarded cenotes as sacred wells. They believed that underground caves and cenotes were portals to the underworld. Gateways through which the souls entered into it.'

'Are you saying that the souls of the dead Maya are roaming about in here?' Randy rolled his eyes with incredulity. 'Are you trying to scare me? Yeah, that sounds really, really scary. Look how terrified I am.' He made a face as if he were very frightened, then laughed. 'The ancient Maya might have believed that kind of nonsense, but I don't. But I have to admit, I'm impressed with your knowledge. You sound more like an archaeologist than a jungle tour guide. How does a guy like you know so much about the ancient Maya culture?'

Ignoring his question, Travis directed the torch beam at the last shadowy corner he had yet to examine, but he couldn't see there anything of interest.

Randy checked his watch. 'Well, it's getting late. We'd better go back. I can't see any other way out. There's nothing to indicate that the dig team has been here. We should go back and try the other passageway.'

'Or maybe we should get out of here and wait for them outside, in the camp,' Travis suggested, feeling a sudden desire to leave this dreadful place. Despite the daylight streaming in from above, there was something dark and oppressive in the cavernous chamber. He couldn't shake the feeling that something or someone was watching them.

'I don't think that's a good idea. They might

be working for hours yet. We should keep looking for them down here. They must be somewhere around, where else could they be? Come on, let's go. We've wasted enough time already.' Randy headed for the exit.

Travis took a step forward, and a sound caught his attention. He tensed, ears straining.

'Wait a moment,' he said.

'What's wrong? What's the matter?'

'I think I heard something.'

Randy paused and turned to face him. 'What?'

He raised his hand, cautioning him to remain silent. 'Listen!'

Nothing. All was quiet. Then, just as Travis was about to move, he heard a light knocking sound, muffled and distant. As before, it didn't last long, and again, silence fell. Both men stood still, not daring to move. They strained their ears, trying to pick up the slightest sound, but nothing happened.

'I think it came from over there.' Randy pointed to the stalactites and stalagmites. 'It was faint, but I'm sure it came from that direction. It sounded like knocking – they must be working close by after all. Who knows, maybe they're just on the other side of that wall. Maybe there's a hidden passage behind those rock formations.' He walked in that direction, shining the torch into the gloom.

Travis didn't move. He waited.

'Yes, just as I thought,' he heard Randy shout.

'There's an entrance to what looks like another tunnel. Come on, hurry up. We'll check it, and if we won't reach them this way we'll go back and try the other corridor.'

Shining his own torch and weaving his way between the intimidating snake figures and the monumental rock formations, Travis joined Randy in the narrow passage.

They advanced with caution, as the stone floor was uneven and there wasn't much room. After a couple of steps, Travis spotted a dark opening in the rock wall ahead.

'Hello, is anyone there?' Randy called again, and they waited for an answer. This time it came right after the echo of his words had faded away: *knock, knock, knock.*

It was stronger than before. More persistent.

Travis got a sinking feeling in his stomach. It didn't sound like men digging – it was more like someone in trouble, desperately trying to attract their attention.

They made their way as fast as they could in the confines of the narrow, low roofed tunnel, towards the noise. With every step the knocking intensified. With every step they were coming closer to its source. To his relief, the passageway soon ended, opening into yet another cavern. Its walls were irregular, with plenty of crevices and niches. A few oddly shaped rock formations divided it into smaller compartments, hiding some parts from direct view.

'There is no one here.' Randy held his torch before him, and advanced into the cave. 'I don't see any—' He broke off mid-sentence, peering into a niche concealed from Travis's view by a large boulder. 'What the hell?!' he exclaimed.

'What's wrong? What is it?'

'Come over here. Quick!'

Intrigued, Travis joined him.

In a far corner, a woman was sitting on the floor, her back against the jagged limestone wall. She was gagged, her hands and feet tied together with a thick rope. As Travis got closer, he noticed there were chains wrapped around her waist and attached to an eyebolt in the wall, restraining her movements. She grunted behind the gag and squirmed, squinting against the harsh torchlight that struck her face.

'Who are you?' Randy stared at her wide-eyed. 'Are you part of the dig team working here?'

She nodded.

Randy turned towards Travis. 'Who did this to her?'

'How should I know? Ask her, not me.' Travis pulled a knife from his pocket and cut the tape wrapped around her head. In one swift movement, he removed the gag from her mouth.

She gasped for breath, then spluttered: 'Help me! Don't just stand there, staring at me as if you've never seen a woman before. Do something! Please, hurry up, before they come back!'

CHAPTER 6

It took a few moments for Randy to recover from his initial stupor. He stood still, studying the woman's face, making no attempt to help her. For a long moment he stared at her lips, noticing how full and sumptuous they were. His gaze slid to her eyes and he was struck by their colour. They were green. Not just plain green, more like smoky emerald flecked with gold dust that sparkled in the bright torchlight each time she moved her head. For a split second they locked onto his own eyes, and he was startled by their piercing intensity. His pulse skittered. Despite himself, he felt an unmistakeable tug of attraction.

'Are you all right?' Travis asked.

Jolted back to reality, Randy turned to his

companion. He was opening his mouth to respond when he saw that Travis wasn't talking to him. Seeing the expression on his guide's face, he stifled a laugh. The poor guy seemed to be even more taken aback by the young woman's striking looks than he was. It was obvious from the way he stood rooted to the spot, gaping at her with puppy dog eyes. And instead of reacting to her pleas for help, he was bombarding her with questions: 'What happened?' 'How did you end up here?' 'Who has done this to you?' 'Where are the others?'

'Of course I'm not all right!' she exploded, squirming uncomfortably and yanking at the heavy chain. 'I've been sitting for I don't know how many hours in a pitch-black cave, attached to the wall like an animal. Would you be all right if you were in my place? Don't just stand there. Do something! Help me! Why are neither of you helping me get out of these?' She pulled at the ropes around her wrists and ankles. 'Help me before those brutes get back.'

She has a fiery temperament, thought Randy. It was one of the qualities he liked in a woman.

'I mean, are you hurt?' Travis said.

'My wrists hurt. The ropes have rubbed my skin raw. Help me get them off.' Her voice rose an octave, reflecting her growing frustration.

Travis rubbed his chin. 'Yeah, you're right. There's no time to lose,' he agreed, sounding more confused than convinced, and with a machete, he cut the ropes that bound the woman's hands and feet.

The woman massaged the reddened skin on her wrists and flexed her ankles. 'Oh, that's much better.' She looked up. 'My name is Chiara. Chiara Carmine.'

After brief introductions, aware they might have little time left, and feeling the need to make himself useful, Randy sprang into action. He inspected the chains, trying to determine how he could attempt to break them. Then he looked around for a rock. He found one that seemed to be both large and hard enough to serve the intended purpose.

'Move this way a bit,' he instructed the woman. She did what he asked her to do. The chain slackened so that a few rings touched the stone floor. He knelt down and struck the links with as much strength as he could muster. He lifted the chain and examined it. The blow had had no effect. There was not even the slightest indentation. He repeated the manoeuvre a few times, but to his great dismay, still nothing happened.

'It doesn't work. I can't break it. Now what?'

'Go and find another piece of rock. A bigger and harder one,' urged Chiara, her impatience audible.

Complying with her orders, he got to his feet, and extending his torch into the gloom, began to move around, searching for a more suitable stone.

'Wait,' Travis ordered, his voice firm, as if trying to make up for his earlier indecision. 'I've got a better idea.' He pulled out his gun, took aim and fired. One of the metal links snapped with a clink.

'Bravo! Well done, that's what I'd call a perfect shot. Come on, give me a hand. My legs feel all numb from sitting in one position for so long.' Chiara struggled to lift her body off the ground.

Travis grabbed her arms, helping her scramble to her feet. She staggered when he released her, then braced her back against the wall. 'Well, I can stand, but I can't do much else with this heavy metal thing around my waist. It's weighing me down. How are we going to get rid of it? You can't shoot it, it's too risky. What if you miss? I don't want to get shot.'

'Don't worry, it won't be necessary. I'll figure out another way to free you.' Travis crouched to inspect the heavy chains around her waist.

Not wanting Travis to get all the credit for freeing the girl, Randy walked over quickly, offering his help.

For the next couple of minutes both men struggled with the restraints. Despite their efforts, they didn't manage to undo them. The chains were too tangled.

'It won't work like this,' Travis said finally. 'We need tools to break the links.'

'Yeah, but all we have is a machete,' said

Randy. 'It's of no use here.'

'And the tools we saw scattered around outside? There were chisels, pickaxes, hammers…'

'It will take too long to go and get them.'

'But how else are we going to break these chains?'

'Wait a moment!' Chiara raised her hand. 'I think the chains have loosened a little. If you loosen them some more, maybe I could wriggle out of them.'

After a few attempts, the chains rattled to the floor and Chiara stepped out of them, a free woman.

'At last.' She straightened up.

Randy couldn't help but notice her shapely figure. His gaze roved over her body, lingering on the soft swell of her breasts and her curvy hips.

She pushed the unruly dark blonde hair back from her face and motioned for them to move. 'Come on, let's go! We have to find the rest of the team and free them too.'

'Then all of you were taken captive?'

'Yes.'

'So where are the others?'

'I don't know. But I saw the armed brutes who captured me go this way. We'd better hurry, they might come back soon.'

'I like your accent.' Randy fell in step beside her. 'Italian?'

'Good guess.'

Before he had time to think of something else nice to say, Travis caught up with them and enquired, 'Who did this to you?'

She took another slug of water from the bottle he had handed to her. 'I wish I knew. All I can say is that we were attacked by a group of brutal and dangerous looking men. I was down in one of the tunnels working, trying to decipher some of the texts on the walls. You see, I'm an epigrapher. I study ancient inscriptions. Two of my colleagues were with me – the rest were busy up in the camp. We were unarmed so we didn't even try to defend ourselves. They caught us all and then left me here alone. I have no idea why. Maybe because I was the only woman. I don't know why they attacked us in the first place. They never said what they wanted.'

'Probably came to rob the place.'

'Could be. I got the impression they've been here before. They moved around the underground with great ease, as if they knew it well.'

'How many of them were there?'

'Six. All heavily armed. We stood no chance against them. They could have easily killed us. I wonder why they didn't.'

'Seems like they had some other plan.'

'Yeah, I guess so.'

A small colony of bats awakened by their presence flew overhead, producing high-pitched squeaks. Up ahead a rather low, arched tunnel opening came into view.

'You sure that's where they went?'

She nodded with a taut jerk of her head. 'They were gone for quite some time, then I saw them again. Briefly. They hurried past without even bothering to check on me.' Her voice was tight with emotion. 'I was lucky you found me.'

Randy clapped her on the shoulder. 'You're with us now. You'll be all right.'

One by one, with Travis leading the way, they entered the tunnel. The ceiling was so low that both men had to hunch over. Being a head shorter, Chiara was able to walk fully erect.

'Maybe we should call out? Your colleagues might hear us if they're somewhere close by,' he said.

'Shh, better to keep quiet. I'm not sure all the attackers left. There could be one or two who stayed behind,' Chiara whispered in reply.

Taking slow, stealthy steps, Randy glanced at the intricate carvings covering the walls. To his untrained eye, they looked similar to the ones they had seen before. The only difference he noticed was that the figures they depicted had become more sinister and threatening. The walls closed in on them the deeper they went, and the still, dank air felt oppressive. Randy could feel the blood pounding at his temples. He hated confined spaces. To his dismay, the tunnel seemed to go on forever, with no end in sight. Sweat began to trickle down his brow and he wiped it off with the back of his hand. He didn't like the way things were unfolding – it was becoming a bit too dangerous for his liking. What he wanted most right now was to get the hell out of there and hide somewhere safe. Struggling to maintain his composure, he tried to look on the bright side. Something positive could come out of it all: a great story. Even better than the one he had originally had in mind. *I could write a fantastic story about my heroic liberation of the archaeological team*, he thought.

'Have you been to this part of the underground before?' he heard Travis ask Chiara in a hushed voice.

'Only once. And I didn't go any further than this tunnel. We haven't explored this section yet.'

'So you don't know the layout?'

'No.'

Three more steps and the tunnel ended. There was another one intersecting it. Tunnel after tunnel. Randy felt like he was trapped in a maze without end. But at least this tunnel was taller and wider, and he could finally straighten up. Apart from the oddly shaped stone figures lining both walls, it looked empty. Before moving any further, the three of them stood still for a while and listened. Nothing. There was no sound to indicate that anyone was close by.

'Which way should we go?' whispered Travis, close to Chiara's ear. *A bit too close*, thought Randy. It was as though he was trying to be intimate with her. And she didn't seem to mind it, she even leaned her head towards him. Was she falling for his rugged good looks? Randy felt a stab of jealousy at the thought that she might be more attracted to Travis than to himself. His vanity was hurt.

'I don't know, whichever. You choose. But I won't stop searching until we find them,' Chiara replied.

Randy noticed that most of the big stone figures they passed depicted snakes. Either alone or two intertwined together, their mouths wide open in a menacing way, as if they were ready to swallow their prey. The light grey or jade green stone they were made from stood out against the coal black of the walls, making them appear even more imposing than they really were. The rest of the statues represented sinister creatures that looked like malevolent demons – part human, part animal – their faces contorted and hideous. He couldn't deny that they were truly remarkable and crafted with a lot of skill, but he had no time to admire them now. That was not what he was here for. He wondered where the archaeologists kept the real treasure, all those valuable and magnificent artefacts he'd been told they'd found here. That's what he would really like to see.

Suddenly there were no more statues, and smooth, black walls rose on each side of the passage, arching above their heads. The floor began to slope steeply downwards into the darkness.

An uneasiness gripped Randy, growing stronger with each step he took. He didn't believe in the concept of an underworld, but if he did, this would be it.

The tunnel widened, opening into a spacious chamber. Travis stopped at its entrance and, shining his torch inside, inspected it.

'Oh, my gosh,' he exclaimed.

Curious, Randy moved closer, and peered over his shoulder. The room was vast but rather low, due to the countless stalactites hanging from the ceiling. His eyes widened as he looked down at the floor. It was littered with human bones and skulls.

'What the hell has happened here?' he exclaimed.

Skeletons of different sizes lay scattered around as if someone had tossed them onto the ground with no respect. Surrounding them were hundreds of pieces of broken pottery.

Randy straightened up. Wanting to show the others that the lugubrious sight didn't scare him, he walked past Travis and ventured deeper into the cavern. Slowly, he swept the torch beam across the walls, revealing more skeletons stuffed into rock crevices. Despite the warm air, he felt a sudden chill, as though icy fingers brushed against his skin. Ignoring the uneasy sensation, he continued to inspect the room, checking each nook and cranny.

All he could see were human remains. The archaeologists weren't here.

Travis and Chiara followed his example and advanced deeper into the cave.

'A mass grave. A truly haunting sight,' muttered Travis to himself.

Randy swept the torch beam across the floor. Up close, he noticed that many of the skulls had been crushed, which meant these people hadn't died a natural death. They had probably been killed by blunt trauma to the head.

'Victims of ritual sacrifices,' whispered Chiara behind his back, confirming his own suspicions. 'Unbelievable. So many children.'

'What happened here? Who broke all those pots?'

'*Huaqueros*, grave robbers?' suggested Travis.

'No,' said Chiara. 'Most probably the ancient Maya. It was common practice after a sacrificial ceremony. They would often smash pots filled with offerings to the gods of the underworld, to release the energy contained within.'

Randy drew a hand across his forehead. 'I've seen enough. This place gives me the shivers. Let's get the hell out of here.'

'There's no other exit. We have to go back. We should check what's on the opposite side of the tunnel,' said Chiara.

Walking at a brisk pace, they soon reached the end of the passageway, where a flight of stone stairs descended into the blackness below.

Another passage to hell? Randy asked himself.

Running one hand along the damp wall and clutching the torch in the other, he placed his feet carefully on each shallow, slippery step, afraid he might lose his footing. He wondered what new horrors awaited them beneath.

When they reached the bottom of the stairs, they edged their way through yet another dank-smelling, winding tunnel. They hadn't got far when the sound of dripping water intruded upon the silence, which until then had been so profound and ominous that it seemed oppressive. They continued down the tunnel until they emerged into a huge chamber with a high vaulted roof, like a cathedral. Shining their torches around, they ventured ahead tentatively.

Here and there were a couple of boulders and odd, man-made stone structures. At the far end, an imposing, red, tapering construction rose up to the ceiling. A broad staircase ran up its centre, leading to what appeared to be a rectangular platform made of yellow-greyish limestone. In the middle of the room was a small, black pool of water.

Randy advanced deeper into the cavern and swung his torch slowly over the walls, which gleamed enticingly. Startled, he moved closer to inspect them. He saw countless shards of what looked like black glass embedded in the reddish-brown rock. They gleamed every time they caught the light. In places, blackened ceramic tubes jutted out of the craggy stone surface. Though they were now empty, he guessed that they used to serve as torch holders. Tens of black, shiny, round, flat objects hung at the height of his chest. The flickering light reflected off their mirror-like surface, casting an ominous glow all around. He swept his hand across one of them. The polished surface felt as smooth and cold as glass. He stared at it. His own, perfectly clear reflection stared back at him.

'What's this?' he asked, astonished. 'Mirrors? But they're so dark? What are they made of?'

'Obsidian.' Chiara walked over and stopped by his side. 'A natural volcanic glass, highly prized by the ancient Maya. The Maya regarded obsidian mirrors as portals to the spirit world and used them as mediums in rituals. The sorcerers who practised black magic used them to communicate with the spirits of the dead or with the gods that had given them the power to see the future or even alter it. By gazing into the smoky depths of an obsidian mirror they could see what was going to happen. It was a medium through which they received messages from the other world.'

'But why are there so many of them here? What was this cave used for?'

'It must have been a sacred ceremonial place. A place where ancient Maya performed secret rituals to communicate with the spirits or to appease the gods of the underworld.'

'Oh, I see, black magic and probably human

sacrifices. That explains why this place has felt so eerily oppressive from the moment we entered it, as if ... I don't know ... as if it were haunted,' muttered Travis.

Randy continued to inspect the rest of the large chamber. 'It's empty. There's no one here.' He didn't try to hide his disappointment.

What he took at first for a pool of black water turned out to be yet another round obsidian mirror embedded in the middle of the floor. He dropped to a crouch in front of it, and was examining the lustrous surface when he heard Travis exclaim, 'Oh, my gosh, that's blood.'

'What?' Randy swung his head around to look up at him.

Travis was standing halfway up the broad staircase leading to the tapering, man-made structure. Eyes wide open, he was staring down at the steps. 'Blood,' he repeated.

'Where? Are you sure? Let me see.' Randy rushed over. The spatter of rusty brown stains on the grey stone did indeed look like blood.

'They hurt them.' Chiara's voice was hushed and tense.

'I don't think it's theirs. It's not fresh. You can tell by the colour.'

Chiara dropped to a crouch to examine the stains more closely. 'Yes, you're right,' she agreed, visibly relieved.

'What is this red stone structure?' asked Travis.

'I don't know. Could be anything.'

'Could they have imprisoned them inside? We should check it.'

Randy climbed the remaining steps and found himself on a rectangular platform. In the middle of it stood a low stone table, splashed with blood. It was dark brown, almost black in colour. At one side of the long slab, he noticed two black stone vessels, both richly stained with blood. There was more blood on the floor.

'An altar? A sacrificial table?' whispered Travis.

Randy nodded. 'Looks like it. And it looks like it has been used by someone other than the Maya.'

'Why? How can you tell?'

'The blood stains are old, but I don't think they are centuries old. More like a couple of months.'

Slowly, Chiara approached the table. 'I hope we're not too late. I hope those brutes haven't killed them.' She paused, her face hardening into an expression of hatred. 'I'll make sure they pay for it if they have.'

Randy shrugged. 'Forget about revenge. At least for now. We should keep looking for them. They might still be alive, and if they are they need our help.'

As if she hadn't heard him, she picked up one of four obsidian knives lying next to the table, her fingers closing tightly around its carved handle.

'Next time we meet, they won't catch me so easily. I'm going to defend myself. Obsidian is the sharpest edge there is. Much sharper than the sharpest steel blade. A perfect weapon.'

'Let's move. Come on. We must continue our search,' urged Randy.

They crossed the rectangular platform and approached what looked like a massive stone door flanked on both sides with two huge jade figures, part snake, part human. It seemed to be the only entrance to the red pyramid. Looking at the walls, Randy noticed that they were covered with carvings of skulls. Row after row of human skulls. Some of them were grinning, which gave the whole thing a ghostly appearance.

'What is this building? A death temple? A tomb?' he asked, but got no answer. Occupied with finding a way to get in, neither Travis nor Chiara paid him any attention. Travis was pushing and knocking at the door, but it wouldn't budge.

'It's closed. How are we going to open it?'

Chiara, who was busy inspecting the walls on both sides of the entrance, looked at Randy. 'There must be a way. An opening mechanism hidden somewhere ...' She leaned closer and, putting her ear against the stone, gestured for them to be quiet. 'I think I heard something. I don't know ... sounded like banging. But I'm not sure. It was hardly audible. There could be someone in there. We must find a way to get inside.'

'Yeah, so keep looking for the opening mechanism. We won't be able to break this door,' Travis said.

'I'll check downstairs. Maybe there's another entrance at the base of this structure,' suggested Randy, and without waiting for their reaction, he scuttled down the stairs.

He shone his torch around, scanning each nook and cranny. The flickering light revealed a dark circular opening in one of the rock walls, just large enough for him to squeeze through. Intrigued, he poked his head inside. What he saw was a smaller cavern, adjacent to the large, cathedral-like one they were in. A mass of stalactites dripped from the low ceiling. The walls were made of glistening crystals, and placed against them were some large masks of crudely carved human heads, partly covered with lichen. Countless human remains were scattered across the floor.

More victims of the rituals? He quickly withdrew his head, not daring to venture deeper inside. *What a macabre place*, he thought. The more he saw of this subterranean kingdom of the dead, the less he liked being there. He had no desire to explore it any further, afraid they might uncover even more morbid secrets of the ancient Maya. He felt it was time to leave. Further search was useless – the archaeologists were probably all dead.

Just then, he heard Travis call, 'Chiara found the opening mechanism. Come on, Randy! Hurry up, we're going in.'

CHAPTER 7

Around the neck of one of the two jade figures flanking the entrance hung a beaded necklace. Its centrepiece formed a large, oval shaped pendant, vivid orange-red and speckled with brown. It was probably made of fire opal, a gemstone highly valued by the ancient Maya.

Travis watched as Chiara traced a finger along its ornate, swirling design. She hesitated, hand mid-air, when she reached the miniature head of a jaguar enclosed in a circle. Then, one by one, she pressed the bulging eyes, and waited. Nothing happened. She pressed the nose, still nothing. But when she pressed the open mouth, the huge stone door shuddered as if it was about to crumble, then slowly slid aside, revealing a pitch-black interior.

A musty odour laced with the faint scent of incense wafted towards Travis. Hesitantly, he took a step forward.

'You'd better wait here. I'll check it out first with Randy.' He wanted to spare her what he suspected might be a gruesome sight.

'Why shouldn't I go with you?' Chiara fixed him with a challenging stare. 'It's better to keep together.'

He didn't insist. Bracing himself for what he might find, he passed through the doorway. An empty corridor with a barrel vault ceiling stretched out in front of him. Clutching the torch in his right hand, he advanced with caution. He had hardly taken three steps when Chiara gripped his shoulder, breathing into his ear.

'Wait.'

He froze. 'What's wrong?'

'Nothing's wrong ...'

And then, she cupped her hands around her mouth and called out, her voice tense with emotion and barely loud enough to reach the far corner of the edifice. 'If you are here, let us know. Don't be scared. It's me, Chiara.'

They stood still for a while, straining their ears, listening. Nothing. Silence surrounded them, profound and unsettling. They waited a little longer, but no answer came.

'They probably didn't hear you.' Randy took a step forward and called out, louder than Chiara had, 'Where are you? Don't be scared. We are friends, not enemies.'

He waited, a hand cupped behind his ear, but his words echoed dully off the vast walls, then faded into silence.

'Nothing,' he declared. 'Not even the slightest sound. They would have heard me, I shouted loud enough. They mustn't be in here.'

Travis advanced deeper. The corridor widened. The ceiling lowered. The ground became even more uneven.

All of a sudden, a biting chill swept over his body, as though an icy breeze was blowing through the passageway. Yet the air was oppressively warm and still. An uncanny feeling of being unwelcome came over him, so strong that it sent further shivers down his spine. He had never experienced something like that before. He suddenly felt strongly that they were treading on forbidden ground. With each step, his uneasiness grew. His stride faltered for a moment, and he shot a quick glance over his shoulder. Chiara and Randy were following closely behind, but their faces turned so that he couldn't see their expressions.

He continued down the passage, the torch shaking in his grip, casting dancing shadows across the smooth walls. Glancing from side to side, he felt his frustration growing. *Where are they?* he thought. After another couple of steps, a half-circular door opening appeared to his left. He dashed towards it and shone his torch inside. The yellow beam swept across the floor of a small square room, illuminating many pots of all shapes and sizes, some richly painted, others carved. Numerous, elaborately crafted clay statues, also brightly coloured or carved, stood among them.

He lifted his torch, revealing multi-coloured murals showing scenes from the lives of the ancient Maya. The finely painted figures seemed to leap and sway in the flickering golden light as he studied them.

He scanned each shadowy corner of the room. It was empty. He shook his head and pursed his lips, trying to suppress the wave of disappointment that washed over him.

Randy poked his head into the chamber. 'Quite a treasure trove in here, isn't it? Pretty impressive. Nice pieces,' he said. 'I bet these things are worth a small fortune.'

Chiara slipped in between Randy and the doorframe. Her face lit up as she glanced around. 'So many offering pots and incense burners. Incredible. I've never seen such a huge collection in one chamber before. And they all look intact. My colleagues would be thrilled...' She sniffed the air. 'I can smell incense. It's quite strong. Someone must have been here not long ago.' She rushed out into the corridor, urging them to follow. 'Come on! We'd better hurry. We've still got a lot of places to check yet. I hope we find them soon. I'm sure I heard someone knocking, so they must be around here somewhere.'

Randy shook his head and sighed. 'Why didn't they answer when we called then? Maybe the knocking was just a rat, foraging around, displacing the stones. Or we got the direction of the sound wrong. I'm telling you, this place is empty. They're not here. We're wasting precious time here, we're searching in vain.'

'How can you be so sure? We've only checked one room. There must be many more, maybe even more levels.' Travis lengthened his stride to catch up with Chiara, who was hurrying down the twisting corridor. He threw a quick glance over his shoulder and saw that Randy was following them, his eyes sending sparks of annoyance from under knitted brows.

The corridor seemed to have no end. It was empty and there were no other rooms.

Strange, thought Travis. He couldn't shake the uneasy feeling that something wasn't right. Something about this place made him wonder if they were walking into a trap. He remembered stories he had read about how the ancient Maya protected burial sites from desecration by constructing elaborate traps that were meant to scare off potential grave robbers. Traps that could cause either instant death or a slow and torturous one. Another cold shiver ran down his spine at the thought of being stuck in a confined space without the slightest hope that anyone would ever come to his rescue.

The corridor narrowed. Somehow the

darkness was getting thicker, closing in on them. Travis's resolve began to crumble, but he resisted the urge to turn around and run out of this dreary, tomblike place.

'I'm amazed at how long this corridor is. The building didn't look that big on the outside,' Randy remarked, jolting Travis from his gloomy thoughts.

'What you saw on the outside was just the front, a small part of the whole structure. The inner corridors seem to run deep into the underground. Who knows, they might even be connected with the rest of the cave system. What I find strange is that we only came across one small room. There must be more. A main burial chamber, for instance. Judging by the number of offering pots and incense burners we've seen, someone very important must be buried here.'

Chiara had barely finished speaking when the passageway widened. Several shadowy niches appeared on both sides. Apart from the brightly coloured murals, all were empty.

Finally, the corridor ended, broadening into a gloomy, vault-like chamber. He stopped and examined it carefully. It was empty.

'Nothing. No other passage. How can it just stop like that?' His voice brimmed with exasperation.

Randy looked at him, eyes flashing anger. 'You see, I was right, they're not here. I told you we were wasting our time searching this place, but neither of you would listen.'

'So now what?' Travis said.

'Let's get the hell out of here. What other choice do we have?'

'Hang on a moment! What's that?' Chiara, brows furrowed, pointed at the right upper part of the wall.

'What? You mean those carvings?'

'Yeah. They are glyphs, the ancient Maya script. Can you shine your torch on the inscription so I can see what it says? It might contain a clue as to what secrets this place is hiding.'

'No time for that now,' protested Randy, pacing back and forth in the restricted space of the room. 'It won't help us find them. We have to get out of here and look somewhere else'

Chiara ignored his outburst and concentrated on deciphering the engravings on the wall, while Travis tried to hold his torch steady. He was impressed by Chiara's tenacity.

As he turned his head, he saw Randy stride over to one of the walls and lean wearily against it. The man seemed to be struggling to contain his temper. His face had grown red with supressed anger, his knuckles clenched white around the straps of his backpack.

Travis moved his attention back to Chiara. He couldn't fail to notice that she was very attractive. His gaze traced the curves of her body. Even the dishevelled sweat- and dirt-stained clothes she wore didn't conceal her shapely figure. In spite of himself, he felt a stir of attraction.

A sound caught his attention, alerting his senses. A swooshing sound. He stiffened, holding his breath, listening. A brief silence followed. Then came another sound. Different this time, like stone grinding against stone. It was low at first, but quickly grew louder. A tingle of alarm coursed through his veins. Suddenly the floor trembled under his feet.

'What's going on?' cried Chiara.

'Bloody hell, the floor is crumbling! Help me!' Randy's panicked screams were mixed with the thunderous crashing and rumbling noises.

Travis spun around. Randy was gone. A large hole appeared where he had been standing. Travis stared at the hole, confused, not sure what had just happened.

'Oh no!' Chiara rushed over and peered inside. 'I can't see him anywhere. Where are you? Are you hurt?' she called, but got no answer.

Travis recovered from the initial shock and hurried to her side. He dropped to a crouch at the edge of the rectangular pit and shone his torch into it. What he saw at first was a thick cloud of dust, and then rolling stones and pieces of timber. Once the dust had settled a bit, he could make out a broad, shallow staircase covered with rubble. Large boulders were blocking one side of it. But he couldn't see Randy anywhere. He craned his neck to get a better view, but still couldn't see him.

'Is he dead?' Chiara asked, expressing his own fears. 'It's my fault. I should have listened when he said it was time to leave.'

'Wait here. I'll go in and look for him.'

'Be careful,' she warned.

Holding tightly to the edge, he lowered himself into the deep, rubble-filled pit. Just as his feet reached the top step, he heard Randy's muffled moans of pain, followed by cursing.

He breathed a sigh of relief, and raising his head up, shouted to Chiara, 'He's not dead!' Then, into the pit, 'Hold on! I'm coming to get you out of there.'

Slowly, he released his grip. Clutching the torch in one hand while the other felt along the jagged wall, he made his way down the flight of steps, carefully placing his feet among the debris. When he was about halfway down the stairs, he saw Randy lying sprawled on his back across a pile of rubble.

'I can't stand up. My arm ... my leg ... this one ... it hurts so bad. Help me,' he implored in a hoarse voice. The leg he pointed to was bent at an awkward angle. Travis knelt down to take a closer look at it.

'Can you move it?' he asked.

Randy's face twisted in a grimace of pain as he flexed his ankle and bent his knee. 'It hurts like hell, but I can move it.'

'And what about your arm? You think it's

broken?'

'No, just bruised. I must have hit it really hard when I fell.'

Out of the corner of his eye, Travis detected movement at the top of the stairs. He raised his head and saw Chiara ease herself over the rim of the pit.

'How is he? How badly is he hurt?' She asked, crouching at his side.

'I don't know.'

Randy gently pulled up his trouser leg, revealing red, bruised skin.

'Oh, you got rather banged up. Will you be able to walk?'

'I'll try.' A grunt of pain escaped his lips as he scrambled to his feet, clutching a large boulder to steady himself. He winced as his weight settled on the injured leg. His good hand on the wall, he descended a couple of steps slowly, limping. Then he stopped and turned to face Chiara and Travis. 'It hurts. But I guess I'll manage to walk. Slowly.'

'You're lucky to be alive,' said Chiara.

'Yeah, I know. I guess it was some sort of a trap. I must have activated it … no idea how, it all happened so fast. The floor moved, and before I realized what was going on, it had collapsed. Next thing I knew I was plummeting down. You're right – I could have ended up dead. It's lucky the trap didn't work the way it was supposed to. That's what saved me. Too much rubble accumulated through the centuries, I guess. So the pit became less deep.'

'What did you do, how did you trigger the trap?' Travis looked at him through narrowed eyes. A trap then, just as he had feared.

With his shirt sleeve, Randy wiped away a trickle of blood from a small gash above his left brow, then dusted off his hair and clothes. 'I told you. I don't know. As far as I can remember, I did nothing in particular. I was standing, leaning against the wall, then I moved … to drop my backpack. Oh, yeah, that was probably it.' He hesitated, looking around. 'Where is my backpack? It must be here somewhere. It must have fallen down with me. I hope my camera is intact.'

They began to search for it. Less than a minute later Travis found it, half-buried under a pile of broken stones and timber.

His fingers shaking, Randy fumbled in the backpack. He pulled out the camera and examined it. 'Oh no, it's broken, just as I feared,' he exclaimed. He clasped his hands over his head. 'What am I going to do now? My splendid photos! I've lost them all. So much work for nothing.'

'Maybe you'll be able to recover some of them,' said Travis.

'I don't think so. And look at the water bottle! It got squashed. All the water is gone.'

'We'd better get going,' urged Chiara.

'Where to?'

'We have to get out of here. You were right, the place is empty.'

'What about the secret passage? Aren't we going to check where it leads?'

'What for? It doesn't look as if anyone has used it recently so there's no need to explore it any further. We'll be only wasting our time. And we've already wasted enough. Come on. Let's go.'

Step by step, they made their way up the stairs.

'Have you got enough strength to climb out of here on your own?'

'I don't know, but I'll have to try.'

Randy tried to climb out, but he couldn't do it by himself, so Travis and Chiara hauled him out.

Once they were all out, they headed straight for the exit.

'Did you manage to read the inscription?' Randy asked Chiara as he limped along behind her.

'No, I didn't have enough time.'

Travis kept silent, as the uneasiness he had felt earlier resurfaced.

Slowly, they rounded bend after bend. When they passed the entrance to the room filled with incense burners, Travis took a deep breath and straightened up. They didn't have far to go now. Only a few more steps and they would be out of this tenebrous place. *At last*, he thought. He continued walking. His torch beam sliced through the darkness, dancing over the rough-hewn stone floor. He lifted the light, aiming it straight ahead. His clammy fingers tightened around the smooth handle, the breath caught in his throat, and he stopped dead in his tracks.

A red stone wall rose in front of him. It looked massive and impenetrable, blocking any further passage. He stared slack-mouthed at where the exit should be, but wasn't. He blinked, his mind spinning. In the profound silence that enveloped the place, he could hear the wild pounding of his heart inside his chest. A cold shiver coursed down his spine at the thought that his earlier fears might have become reality after all. Sweat stung his eyes and he wiped them with his sleeve. He felt a knot forming in his stomach. Inhaling a sharp breath, he said, lowering his voice to a whisper without even realizing it, 'Seems like we are trapped in here.'

'Yeah, the door is shut. Someone has shut it to imprison us. Now what? How are we going to get out of here?' Randy said.

'First of all, we should stay calm. We shouldn't panic.' Chiara wrapped her arms around her chest as though holding herself still. Her face gave no sign but the taut tone of her voice told Travis she was struggling to keep her cool.

'Yeah, easy to say.' Randy shook his head, his eyes gleaming.

'We have to find a way to open the door. There must be something, some device that opens it from the inside.' Chiara moved closer and ran both hands over the rough stone surface of the side walls.

Randy limped to her and touched her shoulder. 'Just hold on a second. What if those thugs who tied you up closed that door? What if they're waiting outside? If we open the door, we might fall right into their hands. It would be a stupid move.'

She turned to face him. 'I don't think anyone has closed the door.'

'Oh no? What, then, you think maybe the wind has shut it?' Travis knew he sounded like a jerk, but felt too edgy to stop himself.

Chiara ignored his sarcastic tone. 'Just let me finish. I think the door closed of its own accord. When Randy opened the secret passage, he must have activated something that shut the main door. A double protection. The ancient Maya wanted to assure that potential grave robbers wouldn't escape punishment.' She paused, then added, 'Better help me look for the opening mechanism. It won't be easy to find as it's probably well hidden.'

For the next couple of minutes they examined the walls on both sides of the door, but didn't find what they were looking for.

'Nothing. And we've searched everywhere. It looks like the door only opens from the outside,' Travis said.

Randy slumped against the wall, panting, his shoulders sagged, then covered his face with his hands and let out a frustrated groan.

Chiara was pacing around, rubbing the nape of her neck. She looked lost and scared. Travis wanted to comfort her but didn't know how. He felt scared himself, but tried not to show it. He kicked a pebble in frustration.

Randy turned off his torch. Instantly the darkness thickened, pressing in around them. The eerie feeling that Travis had experienced earlier intensified. His torch wavered in his trembling hand, sending Chiara's long shadow dancing across the wall but doing little to dispel the gloom.

'Why did you do that?' he asked Randy.

'Do what?'

'Switch off your torch.'

'To save the battery. Why else would I do it? We don't know how long we're going to be in here.'

'Light won't save us. We won't last long without food and water.'

'Thanks, your words are really comforting.'

Chiara straightened up and pushed two sweaty strands of hair away from her face. 'We should do something. We can't just stand here, waiting. The door won't open by itself.'

Randy looked at her through narrowed eyes. 'Do what? Break the door? How? What else can we do? We've already checked everywhere, there's no other way out.'

'No, we haven't checked the whole place,' said

Travis. 'What about the secret passage? We don't know what's at the end of it. There could be another hidden exit.'

Randy blinked but didn't say anything.

Chiara shot Travis a sidelong glance. 'Good idea. You're right, that's where we should look for a way out.'

They set off without delay.

CHAPTER 8

Humberto glanced out of the window of his small private plane, drumming his fingers on the armrests. The dense rainforest canopy spread out below him, like a lush green carpet. Here and there, grey pyramids peaked out of the green, enshrouded in the glimmering golden haze of bright afternoon sunlight. But Humberto barely noticed them. The drab, towering buildings were of no interest to him. They were nothing more than desolate and empty structures. A tourist attraction. Miserable remnants of the earlier splendour of the great Maya empire. A bitter reminder that where now there was dense jungle, had once been the heart of the ancient civilization, with plenty of thriving city-states. Despite being only half-Maya, half-blood, a *mestizo*, Humberto felt a real kinship with the Maya. He shared their traditions and beliefs, and wished he could restore some of the lost glory. Yet, deep down, he knew it was probably an impossible task.

For thousands of years, the Maya people had shaped the land. They chopped and burnt the jungle to clear the land for corn plots or to build market towns and impressive temple cities. They used fire to remove the last year's stubble and weeds from the cornfields that nourished the whole nation, preparing the ground for planting. The summers were blazing with countless fires, pillars of smoke rising to the sky all over the country, the smoky haze obscuring the sun.

That was, until hard times had come, during which droughts and wars ravaged the region, forcing people to abandon their houses and flee to the highlands. The fires went out in the lowlands. The jungle swiftly reclaimed its territory, with trees and underbrush sprouting from the plazas. Thick roots and strangler vines wrapped themselves around the magnificent palaces and temples and made them crumble, bursting through the walls. The snakes, once held in check by the mighty nation, retook the territory, slithering in swarms through the grasses and ferns that grew over the ruins.

Humberto felt angry about the dramatic decline of the once-powerful nation, and so he was trying to take back some of the unclaimed land from the jungle. It was his natural right. He cut and sold the most valuable hardwoods, such as mahogany and cedar. He cleared parts of the forest the way his ancestors used to, turning them to fertile pastures on which his cattle grazed. It was a lucrative business, though a dangerous one, being illegal. But that didn't stop him. He wasn't afraid of taking risks and, besides, he knew how to handle government officials.

Even though the jungle had obliterated almost all traces of the once mighty empire, there were still innumerable treasures hidden beneath the ground. Humberto knew that the ancient Maya had built their palaces and pyramids, the sacred mounds as they used to call them, over earlier structures. He knew that a huge underground realm existed just beneath the jungle floor, with countless secret chambers, passages, tombs and temples filled with splendid pieces of ancient handiwork. It was a magical place. A place filled with powerful energy. A place in which the souls of his long-dead ancestors still lived. He visited it often to perform the same rituals the high Maya priests used to perform to honour and appease the ancient gods, as he believed those rituals would help him achieve success in his endeavours.

Luckily for Humberto, few people were aware of the existence of this secret subterranean world, and so most of the time he was free to roam undisturbed. For years, he had been scouring the place, hoping to find the tomb of a sorcerer from which to draw some special powers, powers that would help him become an even more successful man than he already was. Though he hadn't yet found what he was looking for, he hadn't given up. He was determined to keep looking until he found what he was searching for.

As the plane continued to soar above the jungle, Humberto thought about the group of archaeologists that had turned up about a week ago, and started exploring the site. Their camp was dangerously close to where his cattle grazed, and their presence had threatened to thwart his plans.

It enraged him that these strangers, these *gringos*, had come to his country, thinking they had the right to dig the sacred ground, to desecrate the ancestral remains and rob tombs and temples, removing precious objects and shipping them to museums and art galleries around the world.

How dare they? Who did they think they were? A vein throbbed in his neck and his hands clenched into fists as he thought about it. *Thieves. That's what they were. Common thieves.* He could barely control his anger as the fuming thoughts flashed through his mind. He had known straight away that he had to punish them and make sure the underground world remained a secret. Those men deserved no mercy. They deserved everything that was coming to them.

'We're almost there, aren't we?' asked his

trusted bodyguard, Arturo who was sitting beside him.

Humberto shifted in his seat, feeling the handgun strapped to his thigh digging into his flesh. 'Yeah, we should see the runway any moment now.'

'Good. I can stretch my legs soon.'

Humberto smiled. Every time they were on a plane, it amused him to see Arturo's clumsy efforts to hide the fact that he was afraid of flying. *What an embarrassing weakness*, he thought. How could anyone be afraid of flying, especially someone so strong? Arturo was built like a tank and was capable of killing another human being without hesitation, as he'd proved on many occasions. Humberto studied him for an instant. The poor man sat stiffly, a film of sweat glistening on his forehead and his fingers clutching the armrests so tightly that his knuckles were white.

Since he had discovered Arturo's little weakness, Humberto had taken great pleasure in teasing him, and asked him to accompany him on his plane trips even more often. He paid him well, so he knew Arturo wouldn't decline, and he wasn't scared of repercussions.

Humberto glanced at his golden Rolex watch, then leaned back in his seat, thinking about the deal he had concluded this morning. It was a splendid deal, and he expected to make a lot of money out of it. His tight features relaxed. He ran a well-manicured hand through his raven black, slicked-back hair, and smoothed the sides.

The plane began its descent, swaying slightly. When Humberto looked out of the window again, he saw they were flying so low that the fuselage was almost touching the treetops. A small flock of bright-scarlet macaws flew from a tree, their wings flapping wildly. As soon as they disappeared out of sight, the tiny grass runway came into view.

He patted Arturo on the shoulder and, making it clear from the tone of his voice that he knew his shameful secret, said, 'Bravo, you've survived another one …' He paused, before whispering close to his ear, 'Unless we crash at the last moment.' He sniggered, anticipating the bodyguard's reaction.

Arturo didn't say anything, but looked at him in such a way that if looks could kill, Humberto would be dead.

The plane touched down with a thump. It shuddered and bumped on the grass strip before eventually coming to a stop. Humberto opened the door. A blast of sweltering hot and humid air hit him in the face, before wrapping itself around his body like a heavy blanket.

With long strides, Humberto crossed the clearing and, pushing aside the low-hanging branches and drooping fern fronds, plunged into the thicket. Arturo and Guillermo, the pilot, followed close behind. The trees began to thin out, and the three men found themselves in a sun-beaten grassland.

Humberto approached a barbed-wire fence that marked the borders of his land and prevented the cattle from escaping. He stood there, watching the herd grazing peacefully, a glimmer of pride in his eyes. Then he headed for a scatter of makeshift wooden shacks where the people who took care of his property lived.

A short, sinewy man in his mid-forties emerged from one of the huts. His face was tanned and weather-beaten, his features rough, as though shaped with a blunt chisel. He wore a light-coloured cowboy hat. It was Miguel, the supervisor. Five younger-looking men followed him, all carrying guns slung across their backs.

'Have you caught them all?' Humberto asked, once they were within hearing distance.

'Yes. And we tied them up so they won't be able to escape.'

'Good.'

'They were pretty easy to catch. One of them brandished a knife at me, so I had to stab him. But the others, I mean the men, didn't even try to defend themselves. Only the woman did.' Miguel chuckled, showing his crooked teeth. 'A feisty little creature she was, she fought like a wild cat. She scratched Jairo. She wasn't scared at all, not even when I threatened her with a gun. I tell you, she's got more balls than any of her companions. *Ella tiene cojones grandes como los de un toro!* But she stood no chance against me. I overpowered her easily.'

'I told you not to hurt her.'

'I didn't. I just tied her up and left her alone like you told me to.'

Humberto needed the woman, because he knew she was the one who could decipher the ancient inscriptions. She could help him find the tombs he was looking for.

'And the others, you're sure they won't escape?'

'No way. I checked all the ties myself and—'

'We'd better hurry.' Humberto cut him off, glancing at his watch. 'There isn't much time left to get everything ready for tonight's ceremony. Nothing can go wrong, you understand? Nothing.'

Miguel shrugged. 'I've done what you asked me to do.'

'Why wait for tonight? Why don't we kill them straight away?' enquired Arturo.

Humberto turned around, fixing his eyes with stern intensity on his bodyguard. Clearly, the big guy had more muscles than brains. 'Don't you get it? They have angered the spirits and the gods of the underworld. That's an unforgivable crime. Just killing them is not enough to appease the death gods. What we have to do is make an offering. Open their veins and rip out their hearts. Nothing less will do.' He looked back at Miguel. 'Have you got the dynamite?'

'All we need is in here.' Miguel pointed to the bag strapped across his chest.

'Good. Let's go then. We've got a long walk ahead of us.'

The men didn't dare to disobey, and so they followed him in single file as Humberto pushed his way through the thicket, heading for the entrance to the underground.

CHAPTER 9

One hand on the wall, the other clutching the torch, Travis trudged down the stairs, working his way around the rubble slowly, careful not to trip and fall. When he reached the bottom step, he stopped and shone his light around, illuminating a narrow, rough-hewn tunnel that twisted to the right, descending deeper into the earth.

How deep is it? he wondered. *Where does it lead?*

The jagged walls were slick with moisture and festooned with dusty cobwebs, and the sloping floor was littered with broken stones and dirt. It looked as if no one had set foot in this place for many centuries.

Travis hesitated, then turned to see how his companions were getting on. Chiara was two steps behind, a tense, wary expression on her face. Randy was leaning against the wall, breathing hard. He ran a hand over his face and asked, 'What do you think is at the end of the tunnel?'

'I've no idea. We'll find out when we get there,' said Travis.

'Be careful where you're stepping. Move slowly. There could be another booby trap down there,' Randy cautioned him.

'Trust me, I'm well aware of the dangers. And anyway, you needn't worry, if anything bad happens, this time I'll bear the brunt of it.'

'I wouldn't be so sure. The next one might be more complicated than the first. All of us might get hurt or even killed.'

Travis drew in the thick, musty air and tentatively advanced several steps down the crooked path. His shadow moved alongside him, stretching and lengthening. The only sound was the gravel crunching under his feet. It seemed tremendously loud in the confined space. His shirt, damp with sweat, clung uncomfortably to his skin.

He paused briefly, waiting for Randy and Chiara to catch up, then resumed walking, moving slowly, scanning the ground ahead.

Suddenly, one of his feet slipped, sending a shower of pebbles down the gentle slope. He braced himself against a wall to maintain his balance.

The air grew danker, cooler and more oppressive with every step, but eventually the floor levelled out. Trudging warily, eyes flicking left and right, he rounded a corner.

He continued weaving his way along the crude path, as the tunnel widened. A muffled silence enveloped them, making him feel uneasy. He shot a glance over his shoulder to check that Chiara and Randy were still following. To his relief, they were only a few steps behind. His senses on high alert, he edged around the next corner and shone his light straight ahead.

A limestone wall loomed before him, marking the end of the passage. In the middle of it was a small dark opening. On either side of it stood a large statue of a jaguar, its mouth wide open, baring its teeth and tongue. A thick snake carved out of black granite sat coiled on the back of each feline, head rearing up, ready to strike. Judging by the intimidating stone figures guarding the entrance, whatever lay beyond had to be precious.

'There must be something of immense value in there,' whispered Chiara, echoing his own assumptions.

'I don't care about treasure. All I want to find right now is a way out.' Randy fiddled with the straps of his backpack.

As Travis neared the dark opening, yet another icy chill coursed through his body. The eerie sensation was stronger than the one he had experienced upstairs. He felt the muscles in his neck tense. He hesitated, wondering if he weren't delivering himself into another trap.

But there's also a pretty good chance we'll find the way out, he thought.

He took two more cautious steps and stooped under a low doorway. The beam of his torch pierced the inky blackness, revealing an almost circular chamber. Curious, he ventured deeper into the room. The sound of his boots hitting the polished slabs of stone was startlingly loud, carrying through the confined space and bouncing off the walls.

'Wow!' he exclaimed, glancing around. 'This is pretty awesome.'

Countless pyrite crystals, shining like diamonds, studded the vaulted ceiling above his head more thickly than the stars in the night sky. The sleek walls sparkled, reflecting the torchlight with an opalescent shimmer. A closer inspection revealed that some of them were panelled with polished jade, others with glossy black obsidian. On the opposite side he saw a gigantic obsidian mirror surrounded by a double-headed serpent made of fire opal, the orange of the precious gemstone so vivid that it resembled blazing flames. Next to it stood figures representing several of the Maya underworld gods. Piles of jewellery lay at their feet.

'Amazing!' agreed Chiara. 'I've never seen anything like it.'

Clearly unimpressed, Randy switched on his

own torch. 'There's nothing here. No way out. I don't see any other exit.' He limped around, gazing into the murky corners.

Meandering among the offerings, incense burners, various obsidian tools, jade figurines and pyrite mirrors that lay scattered across the floor, Chiara moved towards a huge stone sarcophagus standing in the middle of the room.

'Looks like we've found the main burial chamber after all,' she said. 'By the looks of it, someone very important is buried here, someone from the upper class. A high priest, a king or maybe a queen.' Her eyes were fixed on the brightly painted sides, as she touched the intricately carved lid.

Randy sighed. 'A royal tomb or not, what difference does it make? I don't care if it's filled with treasure. That's not what we need right now, is it? No amount of gold or precious stones will help us get out of here. Do I have to remind you? What we need to find is a way out. And fast. This burial chamber is a dead end. It's probably been sealed for centuries, to protect all this from intruders. This isn't the way out, we must keep looking.'

Travis swallowed, kneading his fingers together. 'Yeah, but where? We've already looked everywhere and found nothing.'

Randy dragged a hand through his hair, his eyes darting around. 'Don't ask me. All I know is we are stuck in here with almost no water and no food. So if we won't figure out how to get out of this damn place pretty soon, we'll die. And it won't be a peaceful way to go, that's for sure.' Even in the wavering torchlight, Travis could see that Randy's face had become pale.

'I'm not scared. We've got guns and enough bullets to end the suffering whenever we wish.' Travis tried to sound unruffled, but he wasn't sure it had worked.

The truth was, he felt a flicker of fear. The situation they found themselves in was hopeless. He was trying not to think about it because he didn't want to give in to panic. Not yet. There was still a sliver of hope that they might get out of there alive. Only a sliver, no more. Still, it was enough to urge him to act. The chances were slim but there might be a secret passage hidden somewhere behind these walls or under the floor, a passage through which they would be able to get out of this death temple. All they had to do was find the entrance to it. They would have to examine the whole place even more carefully.

He glanced uneasily around the room. Maybe it was his heightened senses, but he felt that threatening, evil presence lurking in the shadows again, watching them. Yet wherever he looked, he saw no one.

Slowly, he walked over to the nearest wall and, running his fingers across the polished, mirror-like surface of the obsidian, inspected it. The volcanic glass had an iridescent, rainbow-like sheen which was incredible to look at, but apart from that, there was nothing there.

'There's someone here.' Chiara's voice cut through the silence, making him almost jolt. It wasn't loud, but it resounded eerily through the murky room.

'Who? Where?' Travis spun around, one hand instinctively moving towards his gun.

Randy was already limping over to Chiara's side, his torchlight piercing the gloom and dust, and dancing around the sarcophagus. 'I can't see anyone,' he said.

'Over there.' Chiara pointed to her right.

Curious, Travis edged closer. He saw a figure slumped near one corner of the tomb, surrounded by ceramic vases and plates with some hardened, unidentifiable substance inside. Was it one of the archaeologists? His heartbeat quickened with anticipation.

As he got closer, he saw that it couldn't be one of the archaeologists. It was a curled-up skeleton with shreds of leather-like skin still attached to the bones. Fine silt and dust coated it. Tattered bits of cloth dangled from the rib cage, and long strands of matted, grimy hair clung to the shrivelled scalp. Pieces of jewellery lay scattered around it – a jade necklace, rings, earrings. It must have been there for centuries.

Randy rubbed the nape of his neck. 'What's he doing here?'

Travis leaned forward, and with an annoyed

gesture flicked wild strands of hair away from his eyes. 'Looks like he, or it could be she – difficult to say now – was buried here alive.'

Randy stiffened, staring at the pitiful human remains. 'Do you think he was a grave robber? And he was trapped inside just like we are now? He died because he couldn't get out?' He paused, then added, an even more nervous timbre to his voice, 'I knew it! There is no way out of here. We won't get out … this is how we are going to end up, isn't it? My boy … my son … he'll be waiting for me. I want to go home, I want to see him again.'

Travis shone the torch across the floor behind the sarcophagus.

'There are two more here,' he exclaimed.

'Really? That makes three. Just like the three of us.'

The other two were smaller and coated with scarlet paint, which made them hard to distinguish from the red-painted pottery among which they were lying stretched out on their backs.

Chiara crouched down beside the first skeleton and observed it for a while. 'I don't think it's a grave robber. It was probably someone who voluntarily enclosed himself inside the tomb of the deceased lord.'

Travis raised his eyebrows in disbelief. 'How can you tell?'

'From the position of the body. The fabric of

the clothes and the jewels that have fallen off the corpse. They seem to be from the same time period as the other items in this funeral chamber.'

Travis moved closer and leaned in to get a better look at the human remains. 'Why do the teeth look so odd?' He pointed at the round green and turquoise pieces in the middle of each frontal tooth.

'Jade and turquoise dental inlays. Only wealthy, noble persons had them.'

'Oh, I see. And what about those two? Why are they so sharp and pointy? That's not normal. They look like vampire teeth.'

'Don't worry, it's not a vampire. The ancient Maya beauty standards differed quite a lot from ours. It may seem strange to us but they found jewelled inlays and pointed teeth beautiful. That's why they often filed their teeth to sharp points.'

'To look like jaguar or snake fangs?' Travis wondered aloud.

'Could be.'

Randy straightened up. 'So if this dead person has jade inlays, it means he or she belonged to a noble family? So why wasn't he properly buried? Why was he buried in here alive?'

'I don't know,' Chiara said, as she started to examine the other two skeletons.

'These ones are so small, they look like children,' said Randy.

'They are children. Both sacrificial victims. I can see cut marks on the rib cages. A few fractured ribs. Probably had their hearts ripped out while they were still alive.'

'That's horrible. How cruel! But why are they so red?' Travis said.

'They're coated with cinnabar. It's a highly toxic mineral that contains mercury. Cinnabar was sacred for the ancient Maya as they associated its red colour with blood, which was a holy substance. They used it for decoration and in funeral rites. Usually for members of the royal family or high priests. Probably to deter grave robbers, as the funeral chambers they were buried in contained many precious objects.'

Chiara stood up, and tucked a loose strand of hair behind her ear. 'Have you got any water left? I'm so thirsty.' Despite the fatigue showing on her face, her eyes burned with a feverish gleam.

Travis fumbled in his backpack and pulled out a plastic bottle. 'That's all there is.' It wasn't much. The bottle was less than a third full. 'Be careful not to drink it all,' he warned, before handing it to her.

'I won't, I promise. Just give it to me.' She raised the bottle to her lips and took a long swig.

Randy licked his lips and reached out his right hand. 'That's enough! Pass it to me. I need some, too. My throat's parched.'

Travis didn't touch what was left, deciding he could go without for a bit longer. It was better to save it. He stuck the bottle back into the backpack and, trying to ignore the dread that clawed at his heart, resumed his inspection of the chamber.

'Still no exit, no hidden passage,' he said, defeated and exhausted. To dissipate some of the pent-up frustration, he kicked at the small stones that littered the floor.

Randy, who was slumped against a wall, lifted his head to look at him. 'Yeah, I told you, but you wouldn't listen. We'd better go back to the main door again and think of another way to try to open it. We might have missed something last time.'

Chiara wrapped her arms around her torso as if she were cold, and mumbled, 'Water ... oh, yes, water ... why didn't I think about it before? That's it. This is the tomb of a noble or royal family, so there should be something here ...'

Travis blinked, rubbing his forehead. 'What are you talking about?'

'Can't you see? She's rambling.' Randy glared at Chiara. 'I told you, there's nothing. It doesn't matter whether the tomb is royal or not. Stop thinking like an archaeologist. We don't have time for this, our priority is to find a way out. Do you understand? It's a matter of life and death! If we ever get out of here alive, you can come back later to explore the place. Now come on. Let's go!'

Chiara didn't move, she just stared at the floor with a puzzled frown.

'Didn't you hear me? Come on,' urged Randy,

limping towards the exit.

'Hold on.' She lifted her head. 'There's something I need to check. The walls and the floor of the tunnel leading to this chamber were damp …'

'Yeah, so what?'

'The water gave me an idea. You see, water was very important for the ancient Maya.'

Randy grimaced. 'What has that got to do with finding the way out?'

Travis rose his hand. 'Just let her finish.'

'According to them, water was where the circle of life began and ended,' Chiara continued. 'They believed that souls must travel across water to enter the afterlife. So to give the king's spirit easy access to the underworld they often built the tombs for their rulers above a spring. As this seems to be a royal funeral chamber, it should be connected through water tunnels with the rest of the underground cave system.'

'You mean there should be another passage accessible from this room, a water passage through which the soul could reach the underworld?' Travis turned to look at Chiara.

She nodded.

'But if so, then where is it? We've checked the whole place and found nothing. I've inspected the walls, the floor, the statues …'

'There is one place we haven't checked yet …' Randy said.

'Oh yeah? Where?'

Randy pointed at the tomb.

'The sarcophagus?' Chiara's eyes brightened. 'I guess you could be right. That sounds logical. A passage running under the tomb which would be accessible through an opening in the bottom of it.'

'Would it be wide enough for us to pass?'

She shrugged. 'I don't know. There is a chance...'

He didn't let her finish. 'What if it's entirely filled with water? We might drown if we enter it.'

'Water was just meant to be a portal to the underworld. So the passage through it shouldn't be that long.' She paused, then added, 'I'm a strong swimmer. I can swim fast underwater. I could go in first.'

Travis walked over to the sarcophagus and ran his hand across the carvings. 'But how are we going to open it? Have you seen the size of the thing? It's huge. The lid alone must weigh a few tons. We won't be able to move it without tools.'

Chiara rubbed the bridge of her nose as if she had a headache. Travis was struck at how fragile and vulnerable she looked at that moment.

'It was just an idea. I thought ...' she muttered.

Randy patted her on the shoulder. 'It's a good idea. It seems impossible but it might actually work. We should try.'

'What if it's booby-trapped?' Travis said.

'Well, we don't have any other ideas, do we?

We don't have much choice,' answered Randy.

'Okay, let's try,' Travis agreed.

The three of them pushed as hard as they could on the heavy flagstone covering the sarcophagus, but it wouldn't even budge. They paused, then tried again, this time using some pieces of wood and what looked like basalt or granite axe blades they found lying on the floor.

Finally, after a few more attempts, Travis felt the lid shift a fraction. Then a bit more. They continued working on it until the opening was a few centimetres wide.

'Let me have your torch,' Chiara said.

Travis handed it to her. She shone the beam into the hole and peered inside. Travis could tell from the look of disappointment on her face that what she had hoped to find wasn't there. He looked inside and saw a red-coated skeleton, a jade death mask affixed to the front of the skull, and multitude of other handcrafted objects lying around the body.

Hesitating, he pointed to the bottom of the sarcophagus. 'Maybe the entrance to the tunnel is underneath it. The body and those artefacts could be lying on a slab of stone and if we move it—'

'No, it's not,' Chiara interrupted. She rubbed her hands on her thighs. 'I thought at first it was. But it's not. It's made from one huge piece of stone. There is no tunnel. The air is dry, not humid.' She dropped to the floor, her back against the tomb. 'I can't stand it anymore. I'm tired. Randy's right, we're going to die in here.' She buried her face in her hands.

Randy didn't say anything, but the resigned look on his face spoke volumes.

Travis sighed and rubbed his temples, trying to fight off the sense of helplessness and despair that threatened to overwhelm him. His shoulders drooped in defeat. He felt drained of energy.

All of a sudden, his torch went out. He shook it and pressed the switch button a few times. Nothing happened. The useless thing was dead.

The gloom around them thickened. Randy's light was too weak to chase much of it away. They had little time left to act. Soon they might run out of light altogether.

The problem was, Travis had no idea what else they could do, where else they should look for an exit. He shuddered as the harsh realization sank in that there was no way out of this grim place. They were trapped, and they were going to die in there.

CHAPTER 10

A sharp pain in his left thigh jolted Greg awake. He opened his eyes but couldn't see a thing in the inky blackness that surrounded him. Not even a speck of light. He blinked, but still, could see nothing. The blackness was as thick and profound as before.

His breathing quickened and his heart started to pound wildly in his chest. *Have I lost my sight?* he wondered. *What happened? Why can't I remember anything?*

Cold seeped into his body from the hard, rough ground beneath it. There was nothing to protect him from it. Where was his sleeping bag? Where was *he?* Clearly not in his tent. He wanted to rub his eyes, but to his consternation, he couldn't lift either of his hands, as both arms were pinioned to his sides with ropes. Ropes also bound his ankles. He tried to wriggle free, but the ropes tightened even more, digging into his soft flesh. Ignoring the pain, he rolled onto his side and pulled his knees up to his chest, trying to get to a kneeling position. Finally, after a few futile attempts, he managed to do so but was unable to hold his balance. Frustrated, he rolled onto his back, cursing under his breath.

Who had done this to him? And why? His head felt groggy and he couldn't think straight.

Then, all of a sudden, images flooded into his mind, images of himself and his colleagues working in the underground. Daniel, Ramiro and Antoine were with him in the secret passage they had discovered when, out of nowhere, a group of men had appeared in front of them. They were hostile and heavily armed. Taken by surprise and unprepared, Greg and his colleagues didn't even try to defend themselves. It was clear that they were outnumbered, and they didn't stand a chance.

The men had taken them through a maze of tunnels and caves to a part of the underground they didn't know. There, they had tied them up and injected them with something. That was the last thing Greg could remember. The recollection made helpless anger twist and coil inside him. He gritted his teeth.

He had no idea how long he had been lying there, on the cold cave floor. Maybe a few hours. Or maybe more than a day.

So, Daniel, Ramiro and Antoine should be around

here somewhere, he thought.

He listened, straining his ears. Apart from the faint sound of dripping water, the place was as silent as a tomb.

'Hello?' he called softly. He waited for a response but none came. He rose his voice an octave. 'It's me, Greg. Are you here? Daniel? Ramiro? Antoine? Guys, answer me!' Again, nothing. He was getting more and more nervous. Were they still unconscious? Or worse, dead? Was he all alone here, deep in the underground? He tried to stay calm and not let panic take over.

And what about the others? Had Chiara, Juan, David and Kevin also been attacked? Maybe they had managed to escape and would come looking for their missing colleagues? *Not much chance of that*, he decided. They wouldn't be able to look around with the attackers roaming around. He would have to get out of here on his own. And he had to hurry. The attackers might change their minds and come back to kill him.

But almost immediately, doubts started to enter his head. Even if he managed to free himself from the ties, how, in such an immense underground maze of tunnels and caves, was he ever going to find a way out, without a torch, without anything to guide him? It seemed like an impossible task. He would get lost for sure. He felt resignation take hold for a second, before his survival instinct kicked in, urging him to act. Yes, he had to try to escape. He couldn't just sit and wait. Wait for what? Death? It would be better to die trying to escape than from thirst or hunger, or at the hands of those brutes. And anyway, there was a chance, however small, that he might find the exit.

He had a vague memory of the cavern the assailants had brought him into. He remembered seeing a low ceiling and irregular, jagged walls. If only he could find a sharp enough edge to rub the ropes against, they might break. With great effort, he managed to rise to a sitting position and shuffled clumsily, having no idea where the wall was.

Finally, after what seemed like ages but was probably a couple of minutes his back hit cold stone. A wall? He pressed harder. Yes, it was a wall. He rubbed against it, but to his dismay he couldn't feel any edges sharp enough. Slowly, he moved along it, searching further.

Suddenly, one of his legs hit something soft, something that felt like a body slumped against a wall. A dead body? His instinct was to recoil, but he quickly composed himself and moved closer.

A muffled sound reached his ears. A soft moan. Then Greg felt the soft shape next to him move. Relief swept over him.

'Hey. It's me, Greg,' he said. 'Wake up! We have to get out of here.'

'What? Where?' He recognized the voice, though it was only a dazed mumble.

'Daniel? Are you all right? Can you move?'

'I've got a splitting headache … can't see anything.'

'Don't panic. And don't make too much noise. I don't know if those men have gone, and even if they have, they might come back. Somehow we need to free ourselves, get out of here and find somewhere safe to hide.'

'Where are we? What the … I can't move my hands. And my legs are bound.'

'I can't help you there. Mine are tied too. I was looking for something sharp to break the ropes. Do you remember what happened?'

'I can hardly think. Wait, yeah, I think I remember—'

'Daniel? Greg?' another voice called weakly from the opposite side of the cave.

'Antoine! You okay?'

'I can't move.'

'Are you close to the wall?'

'No idea. Where are we? Why is it so dark? My arms hurt. I need to get rid of these ropes …'

Greg heard what sounded like some dislodged stones rolling, followed by the thump of something hitting the ground. He heard a voice cursing angrily. It was Ramiro.

His heartbeat quickened with excitement. At least the four of them were still alive.

'We need to find something to break these ropes with,' he said and continued his search for a sharp edge, but he couldn't find one sharp enough. With the sharpest he found, it would have taken hours of rubbing to break the ropes. Hours he didn't have.

So he kept searching, his impatience growing. Then, just as he was about to roll onto the ground and cry in frustration, he felt a knife-like stone. This was exactly what he needed! With renewed energy, he began to rub the ropes wrapped around his wrists against the protruding piece of rock, careful not to cut his skin in the process.

He felt beads of sweat trickle down his temples from the effort. Eventually, the ropes became slack, then snapped, and one by one they fell to the ground. He wriggled his hands free, lifted them to his face and flexed his fingers. They felt a bit stiff, but he could at last move them freely. A surge of hope washed over him. He leaned down to untie his ankles. Impatient, fingers shaking, he fumbled at the tight knots.

'Greg?' he heard Daniel say.

'What?' He lifted his head.

'In my pocket … I've got a cigarette lighter, but I can't—'

'Well why didn't you say so before?!' Indignation heightened his words. 'I can get it, my hands are free.' He moved towards the sound of Daniel's voice.

'Where is it?' he asked when he finally reached him.

'Here, the left trouser pocket.'

He fumbled about in the dark for a while,

then felt his fingers close around the cigarette lighter, and his lips curled into a smile of triumph. 'I've got it!' He pulled it out and flicked it on. A small orange flame popped up and danced in the darkness, illuminating Daniel's face. He looked straight at Greg, a glimmer of hope in his eyes.

'Help me. Burn the ropes.'

'What if I burn your skin?'

'Just take care not to. See the tail next to this big knot? Set fire to it. It will burn the knot without doing much damage.'

Greg did as he said. It worked, and Daniel was free.

Next, he lit the loose end of the rope around his ankles and waited for the flames to consume the tangled cords. The ties broke. He staggered to his feet and took a few unsteady steps, holding the lighter in front of him. The flickering light was so feeble, he could barely see. Guided by the sound of their voices, Greg found Antoine and Ramiro, and using the lighter, he burned through the ropes that tied them as he had done with Daniel's.

He ventured deeper into the cave, his eyes straining to penetrate the blackness ahead. As they adjusted to the gloom, he lowered the flame to look at the floor. He saw several skeletons scattered around him. Behind one of them he could make out a dark form. A boulder? He moved closer. When only a step separated him from the dim shape, he saw it wasn't a boulder, but another body. He dropped to a crouch beside it, directing the light at the face.

'Hey guys, I found Kevin.' He shook his colleague, who grunted in response.

'There's someone else here too,' he heard Daniel say.

'Who is it?'

'I can't tell without the light.'

'Alive?'

'Yeah, he's breathing, but unresponsive.'

Greg walked over to him and bent down to look at the face. 'Hey, that's David.'

Glancing to his left, he spotted a third body. He gasped when he touched it. It was cold and stiff. Gently, he turned it over, and Juan's glassy eyes stared at him. Empty. Dead. There was a large blood stain on the front of his shirt.

'Bastards!' He balled his hands into fists, seething with rage.

'Why did they kill him? He wasn't armed,' Daniel muttered, his voice full of consternation. 'Come on, hurry. We need to get out of here. Fast. Otherwise we'll end up dead too.'

'And what about Chiara? She's the only one we haven't found.'

'Then she isn't here.'

'What do we do with them?' Antoine had joined them, and he nodded towards Kevin and David. 'We can't leave them here.'

Greg shot him an impatient glance. 'Try to untie them while I look for a way out.' He lit a piece of rope and, holding it in front of him, inspected the rest of the chamber. He could see better now as the flame was bigger and gave more light.

'There are two tunnel openings going in opposite directions,' he said. The blazing piece of rope had started to burn his fingers, and he dropped it to the ground.

Antoine looked at him. 'I only untied the ropes around the ankles. I can't undo the other ones. They're still unconscious, so I don't dare burn the knots.'

'Don't bother. It would take too much time and time is what we don't have. We must leave right now, find a safe place to hide. The cigarette lighter won't last long.'

'We'll have to carry them then.'

'It will be too difficult. Some of the tunnels are very narrow,' said Ramiro.

'We won't need to drag them the whole way. We can hide them somewhere safe,' Daniel replied.

'No, we shouldn't leave them.'

'We'll be too slow if we don't. We'll never manage to get out of here.'

'They might wake up soon and then they can walk.'

'And if they don't …?'

Greg stiffened. 'I think I heard something.'

'What?'

He put a finger to his lips. 'Shh! Listen!'

They all fell silent and listened, ears straining to catch the slightest sound. Apart from the distant dripping of water, all was quiet.

Greg shrugged. 'I thought I heard a muffled thud. Like a stone falling, or something heavy. I'm not sure. It seemed quite far away. But I might have imagined it ... Anyway, we'd better hurry. Our attackers might come back soon. If we linger too long they'll catch us and probably kill us. Come on, let's go.'

Carrying the two unconscious bodies, they headed for one of the exits.

'You sure that's the one we should take?' asked Daniel.

'I don't know. They both look the same to me. I have no idea which direction we came from, so let's just take this one.' With one hand holding the lighter and the other feeling along the wall, Greg stepped into a dank smelling tunnel. He walked cautiously, the small flame barely lighting his way. He had no idea where he was, nor where the passageway led. He had nothing to guide him.

'Too slow, walk faster!' Antoine's impatient voice echoed through the darkness.

'I can't go any faster, I can hardly see where I'm putting my feet.'

'We won't make it if we don't hurry.'

Greg quickened his pace and walked around a sharp bend. The tunnel narrowed until both his shoulders touched the walls. The ceiling was so low he had to stoop. The air became more humid. Water trickled down the smooth walls.

He stopped.

'What's wrong?'

'I think we took the wrong passage. I don't remember walking through such a narrow tunnel.'

'What now then? Should we go back and try the other one?'

'No, it's too late. We'll have to carry on.'

'There might be more than one way to the exit.'

'Or we are moving deeper into the underground.'

'What if we get lost?'

The small flame wavered, and Greg winced as it licked his finger. And then it was gone. Blackness surrounded them. He flicked the lighter once, twice. Sparks flew. Then a timid pale-blue flame flickered briefly. He flicked the lighter again, and then again, but nothing happened.

'It's dead,' he said, and cursing under his breath, he threw the useless lighter to the ground. He breathed deeply, trying to keep the rising panic under control. They still had no choice but to move ahead, so he ventured deeper into the passage.

The tunnel widened and turned to the right. He felt the floor slope downwards at a sharp angle. He leaned further into the wall and walked even more guardedly, but it didn't stop his feet sliding on a wet patch. He began to glide, and an anguished groan escaped his lips. Frantic, he dragged his hand along the wall in the hope of finding something to grab hold of and stop his fall. But there was nothing. Suddenly, he was in water, his arms splashing wildly, struggling to keep him afloat.

A few loud thuds, then the sounds of splashing and cursing told him that his companions had ended up in the water too.

After the initial panic had passed, Greg realized that the water was shallower than he had feared. His feet reached the bottom and his head and shoulders still rose above the surface. But it was icy cold. He shivered, feeling the cold seep into his bones.

Daniel's scared voice reached him through the darkness. 'We're trapped. There's no way out.'

Greg drew a deep breath. 'Stay calm, don't panic. If we stay calm, we'll find a way out.' He tried to sound reassuring, but his voice faltered. The truth was, he didn't believe they would make it out of here alive

CHAPTER 11

His attention focused on the path ahead, Humberto threaded his way through the dense undergrowth. He hated walking in the jungle. It was difficult, even for someone like him who knew the jungle well. He pushed aside large drooping fern fronds and dangling creepers, cursing under his breath. Even though he'd been here many times before, he struggled not to get lost among the lush vegetation.

'We're almost there,' he heard Miguel say. The old man must have detected his growing impatience.

The oppressive humidity slowed down Humberto's movements and made him feel irritable. After having spent several weeks in the Highlands, he still wasn't used to it. He paused to drink some water. His thirst quenched, he continued weaving through the thicket. Plants grew with such speed in this hellish place that trails disappeared within less than a couple of days. If not stopped by men, the rainforest would in no time engulf everything in its path, erase all trace of civilization.

Finally, the faint trail became more defined, and he recognized where they were. Miguel was right, they didn't have far to go.

They emerged into a clearing and, squinting against the bright sunlight, Humberto pointed towards several tents pitched around the edge. 'That's their camp?'

'Yes.'

'You'll have to clear it later. Erase all trace. You sure you've got them all?'

Miguel nodded. 'Yeah, sure as hell. We watched them for a while before we decided to attack. Watched every move.' He chuckled. 'And they were so dumb they didn't suspect a thing.'

Humberto glanced at his watch and yawned. 'No time to waste. Come on, let's go. Show me where they are.'

They headed for the underground, Miguel setting a brisk pace. As soon as they entered it, a sepulchral silence surrounded them. The air changed. It became heavier and thicker with a dank, earthy smell. Humberto didn't mind it. He felt close to his ancestors here, believing that this was where their souls lived.

For several minutes the men weaved their way in silence through the twisting maze of gloomy tunnels and chambers. They were about to round another corner, when Miguel asked, 'Do you want to see the woman first?'

'Not now. I'll need her later, to tell me what the inscriptions on the red temple say. But first we've got to make offerings and sacrifices to all the gods of the underworld. If we don't, they'll get angry and punish us for disturbing the peace of the dead.' He swallowed loudly. 'Show me where the men you've caught are. I want to see them before we get everything ready for the ceremony.'

'Wait a moment, I'll just check on her. We aren't far.'

He shot Miguel an annoyed look. 'I told you, not now. No need to waste our time. We've got better things to do.'

Miguel's wizened face screwed up into a frown, but he didn't argue.

'Where are they?' Humberto asked, as they crossed the spacious room with a cathedral-like ceiling and mirrored walls.

'This way.' The old man nodded towards a dark opening at the opposite end of the cave.

Humberto glanced at the red temple, half bathed in shadow. *We'll have to find a way to open it*, he thought. *It must be full of treasures.*

One more tunnel, a short one. And another chamber.

Suddenly Miguel stopped, listening.

'What is it? Is something wrong?' Humberto looked at him concerned.

Miguel pointed to the dark opening in the middle of the opposite wall. 'We've put them there, in the next room. But it's so quiet, I can't hear anything.'

Fabio, a strongly built, young man who they called Stone Face, as he never smiled and was rather close-mouthed, spat chewing tobacco juice on the ground and said, 'Means the drug hasn't worn off. They're still out cold.'

'Or they're awake, heard us and are so scared they don't dare make a sound,' Arturo said.

'Or maybe they're dead.' Humberto wagged an angry finger at Miguel. 'You weren't careful. The drug you used was too strong. This is not good at all. I wanted them to be alive for the ceremony.'

'Don't worry. I'm sure I didn't give them enough to kill them,' assured Miguel, and he advanced towards the arched opening in the limestone wall on the other side of the room.

Humberto followed. The entrance was so low that he had to bend his head to pass through it. He looked around the cavern slowly, using his torch, and felt a rush of blood to his head. He took a deep breath, held it for a moment and let it out slowly, then fixed Miguel with a stare, his eyes narrowed to glittering slits. 'There's no one here. The place is empty. Where are they? Where have you put them?'

'I … I … I don't know … I don't understand …' the old man stammered, a look of utter disbelief on his face.

'There's nothing to understand. Just show me where they are.'

'Here. This is where we left them.' He motioned at the ground by one of the walls.

He clenched his hands into fists, until the nails bit into the soft flesh of his palms and his knuckles went white. 'Here? There's no one here. Where are they?' he repeated, uttering each word slowly.

Miguel scratched his ear. 'I … I don't know.'

'There's someone here,' called Luis, a stocky, broad-shouldered man with a thick moustache and bushy eyebrows. He was crouching in a far-off corner, peering behind a rock outcropping. 'It's the one you stabbed. He's dead.'

The body was wedged between the wall and the outcropping.

'Are any of the others there?' Humberto shouted.

'No, just him.'

Fabio leaned down and picked something up from the floor. 'Look at this.'

'What? Let me see.' Humberto looked at the piece of rope Fabio was holding. 'Looks like they've escaped, doesn't it?'

Miguel was walking around, glancing into each nook and cranny, cursing and muttering. 'I don't get it. How? How did they manage to free themselves? The knots were so tight. I checked them all myself.'

'No time to think about that, we must find them. We can't let them get away.' Humberto pulled out his gun.

The others followed his example, grabbing their weapons.

Miguel stopped pacing. He straightened his shoulders and swallowed hard. 'We'll get them. Without a light they couldn't have gone far. And they must be still under the influence of the drug. Too weak to walk fast. I swear, I'll find them.'

Humberto tightened his grip on the pistol. 'You'd better pray they haven't got far. Otherwise *your* blood will flow on the sacrificial altar. It will be *your* heart that I will rip out and offer to the gods.' He pointed at the dark opening looming straight ahead. 'There are two more exits. We have to check both. I'll search this one. You, Fabio and Arturo come with me. The rest, go check the second tunnel.'

He crossed the room and entered a narrow, winding passageway. Shining his torch at the floor, he examined it closely. He saw prints in the wet earth and gravel, several sets of boot prints. And they all looked fresh. He turned to Miguel, who was right behind him. 'You and your men haven't walked through here recently, have you?' he asked, lowering his voice to a whisper.

'No, not for a few weeks. When we brought

them here, we left the same way we came.'

'So it must be them. This is where they went. There's no need to search the second tunnel. Call the others, tell them we need them here.'

He waited for Miguel to come back, then advanced deeper into the tunnel. They walked in silence, listening, straining to pick up the slightest sound. But the only sounds Humberto could hear were the gravel crunching beneath their feet and the relentless drip of water down the jagged rock walls.

The floor began to slope downwards, forcing him to slow his pace. He placed one hand on the wall for support and looked more closely at the ground. There were some unusual marks in the wet soil. They looked like they could have been left by bodies sliding downward with speed.

Suddenly, the tunnel opened into a large, low-roofed cavern, filled almost entirely with water. He stopped at the edge of the pool and shone his torch across its smooth surface. The crystalline green and blue water was so clear that he could see to the bottom of it. It was empty. He shone the beam over the limestone walls surrounding it. Again nothing.

'Where are they? This placc is empty.' He looked at Miguel. 'The footsteps don't lie. They went this way. There must be another exit.'

'Not that I know of.'

'So what are you waiting for? Go and check!'

'But … the water …'

'The water? Don't tell me you are afraid of water.'

'I can't swim. I don't—'

'Water doesn't scare me. I'll go and check,' cut in Fabio, and before Humberto had time to react, he had lowered himself into the pool.

Seeing that it was only waist-deep, Miguel followed. Humberto smiled at the old man's pathetic attempt to save face.

Humberto remained where he was, watching the two men wade through the water towards the opposite shore. There was a stone ledge running along the other side of the basin, big enough to stand on. After a few failed attempts, Fabio and Miguel climbed onto it and began to examine the wall.

He shook his head and let out an impatient sigh. The two men moved at a snail's pace. It would take them forever to inspect the whole wall at this rate. He turned towards Arturo.

'Go and help them. And hurry. We've wasted enough time.'

He returned his attention to Miguel, and saw him disappear behind a protruding boulder. Seconds passed, and he didn't reappear. *Strange*, he thought. *Is there another passage after all?* Then he heard a thud, and what sounded like a cry.

'What's going on? Have you found them?' he shouted, but got no answer.

He gestured at the remaining men standing by his side. 'Come on. He might be in trouble.'

He descended into the pool and, holding his gun tightly, pushed his way through the water. He was about halfway there when he saw Miguel re-emerge from behind the boulder. A smile played at the corners of the old man's mouth.

'I found them,' he yelled, gesturing, hardly able to contain his excitement. 'There's a small cavity behind this boulder, which they have crawled into. A dumb move. There's no other exit, so they can't escape us now. They're trapped.'

CHAPTER 12

Travis felt fear tighten around his chest like an iron band. He could hear his heart hammering in his ears and his mind clouded over with gloomy thoughts. They were trapped. Entombed forever. He couldn't lie to himself anymore: there was no way out. They would die in here, and it wouldn't be a peaceful death. His shoulders drooped in resignation and he slumped against the wall.

But yet again, just when he'd given up all hope, his sharply honed survival instinct took over, urging him to keep going. There was no point sitting and waiting for death to come. It would be better to do something. Anything. At least try to escape.

He briefly contemplated Randy's suggestion

of trying to open the main door of the temple again, but he quickly rejected this idea. They had tried many times already. He just didn't believe that they'd find a secret opening mechanism. Maybe there wasn't one. Surely they would have found it if there was, as they had left no stone unturned in their search. Right away doubts assailed him. But maybe they should inspect the whole place again, just in case. Being rattled as they were, maybe they had missed something. Who knows, they might have more luck this time. He wavered, unable to decide what to do. Chiara's words about the ancient Maya death beliefs echoed in his mind. It was quite possible that there was a secret passage hidden somewhere in the vicinity of the tomb.

He rubbed his temples, feeling exhausted all of a sudden. A muffled silence filled the burial chamber. It felt oppressive, to the point of suffocation. He drew a deep breath and lifted his head to see what the other two were doing. Randy was leaning against the wall, clutching his hair, rocking slightly. Chiara sat on the floor close to the sarcophagus, hugging her legs, her head resting on her knees. Both of them looked exhausted too, as if they had given up all hope and succumbed to despair.

Travis picked up Randy's torch and, sweeping the light slowly across the floor and walls, he gazed once again around the gloomy chamber, taking all in. The sarcophagus. The burial offerings. The three human skeletons. The smooth, glossy walls. The double-headed serpent-framed mirror. The sinister-looking statues representing Maya deities of the underworld. The statues caught his attention. *Maybe we didn't examine them well enough*, he thought. *Maybe there's something hidden in them, like in the two jade creatures flanking the main entrance to the temple.* He walked over to the figures and ran his fingers over the carved stone, probing each recess and each rise.

'You won't find anything there,' Randy said, making him turn. 'I've already examined both of them. Found nothing. I'm telling you, there's nothing here, in this room. No hidden exit. It's just a simple burial chamber that has been sealed off for centuries. Listen to me, we're wasting our time, lingering uselessly down here. We should go back to the main door and search there.'

'Not yet,' said Travis through clenched teeth.

'Not yet? Why not?' Randy's features hardened to iron. He moved closer. He shook his head, a scowl of indignation twisting his face.

'Because I don't believe we'll manage to open the door. Because I think there's a greater chance we'll find a secret passage here.'

Randy shot him another glaring look and said, his voice rising almost to a shout, 'I told you, there's nothing here. No exit. Why won't you listen? Why are you so stubborn? We have to look somewhere else. Don't you get it? It's a question of life and death. Do you hear me? Life and death! So hurry up! The torchlight might go out soon, and it's the only one we have. What then? How are we going to find a way out without a light? Have you thought about that?'

Travis held Randy's angry gaze, unblinking. 'Hey, don't take that tone with me! I don't need you to tell me what to do. You listen to me now. I'm not done here yet. I need to check a few more things.'

'Check what? There's nothing to check.'

'Stop arguing!' Chiara scrambled to her feet and walked over to them. 'It's not helping.' She paused, then shook her head and hugged her arms as if she were cold. 'There should be something—'

Randy didn't let her finish. 'What? You too? Don't start that again. I've had enough. We need to go to the main door to—'

'Really?' she interrupted. 'If you're so sure, why don't you go? What are you waiting for? You're free to do what you want. Nobody's holding you here.'

'Alone? I can't. We've only got one torch. We can't split it, can we? And my leg, my shoulder … it hurts too much. You know very well I wouldn't be able to climb out of the shaft alone. Why do you insist on searching here? There's nothing. You are just as obstinate as he is.'

'And you're a real pain in—'

Travis clasped his hands over his ears. 'Stop it! Stop arguing. We need to think where else we should look.'

The tone of his voice silenced them both.

Travis continued to inspect the statues, but found nothing. All his energy drained away. He leaned against the wall, his face buried in his hands.

Chiara walked up to him. 'Give me the torch. I want to check the floor.'

'Why? I've already checked it.'

She pushed a few stray strands of hair away from her face, tucking them behind her ears. 'Yeah, but you could have missed something.'

He crossed his arms. 'What do you expect to find that I might have missed?'

She bit the corner of her bottom lip, her gaze darting around the room. 'I don't know. Something. Anything. I just can't stand waiting, doing nothing.' She hesitated, then drew in a long breath and expelled it. Looking him straight in the eyes, she said, her voice hardly above whisper, 'The truth is, I'm scared. I don't want to die in here.'

Travis wanted to say something reassuring, but he couldn't think of anything, so he remained silent. He handed her the torch, then pulled out the bottle of water from his backpack. He took two small sips, which was all that was left. It was too little to quench his thirst, but just enough to take away the dry feeling in his mouth.

Chiara walked around the chamber shining the beam across the floor, her dark eyes scrutinizing each depression and protrusion. When she neared the sarcophagus, she dropped to a crouch to take a closer look at some of the pottery.

Randy, hands jammed into his pockets, followed her with a half-hooded gaze, his head cocked to one side. Annoyance flickered across his face when he saw her examine a pot. 'What are you doing now? Studying a pot? What a waste of time! What's wrong with you? Have you lost your mind? You think an old pot will help us find a way out?'

Chiara lifted her head. 'I've found something. There are traces of burning, probably from the use of incense.'

'So what? That's your great discovery? Are you mad? We don't have time for this now.'

She stood up and rolled her shoulders. 'What I just found proves my theory that there is a secret passage leading out from this chamber.'

'Oh, yeah, really? How's that?'

'The amount of sooty residue tells me that the incense was burnt more than once. I believe people came here to perform rituals for many years after the burial. Probably high priests and family members. And they used some secret passage to re-enter the tomb.'

'Okay, I get it. Interesting piece of information. But it still doesn't bring us any closer to finding where it is.'

'No.'

'So we are back to square one. We don't have

the slightest idea how to get out of this creepy place. We are trapped.'

Chiara gave a half shrug. She turned her back on Randy and took a step or two in the opposite direction. The torchlight moved with her, picking out of the shadows one object after another. Travis swivelled his head to keep her in view. The light wavered, then fell on the large, smoky-black mirror encircled by the twisting body of a double-headed snake made of fire opal. It reflected off the smooth surface of the obsidian, making it shimmer and twinkle. As he watched the iridescent sheen, something began to nag at the back of his tired mind. He blinked and scratched his chin, feeling flustered. Then, suddenly, he knew.

'Why didn't I think of it earlier? The mirror …' he muttered, moving closer to it.

Chiara jerked her head in his direction. 'What?'

'The mirror,' he repeated.

'What about it?'

'The ancient Maya believed mirrors had magical powers, that they were passages for supernatural forces, right? That's why they used them in rituals. Mostly to communicate with spirits or to see the future. And, from what I remember, they associated them with water. A bowl of water or a smooth surface of a water pool, similar to a mirror, served them to connect with the spirit world.'

'Yes, that's true. Go on.'

Randy rolled his eyes. 'I don't see what it has to do with—'

Travis continued, unperturbed. 'For the ancient Maya, water-filled sinkholes were portals to the underworld. And the smooth, reflective surface of a mirror was a doorway to another realm. I don't know, it's just an idea. But there could be something in the mirror.'

Chiara shifted from one foot to the other. 'You mean the obsidian mirror could be hiding a secret passageway? That is where you think we should concentrate our search?' She hesitated, staring at it. 'Yes … you could be right. It sounds plausible. And there should be something, some device, that unlocks access to it.'

'Yeah …'

Randy sighed. 'As if it were so simple! It might be so well-hidden we will never find it. We'll only waste more precious time.'

Chiara moved forward, gesturing to him. 'Come on. What are you waiting for? You'd better help us look for it.'

A scornful shake of the head was Randy's only reaction.

Chiara and Travis examined the snake figure twisting around the mirror and the wall surrounding it. Randy remained standing where he was, watching them from a distance through hooded eyes.

They found nothing. Not willing to give up so

easily, they re-examined everything. Again, nothing.

'It was just an idea,' Travis said, unable to keep the disappointment out of his voice. His shoulders sagged in defeat. 'But I guess I was wrong.'

Randy moved closer, glaring at him. A muscle in his jaw twitched. 'We've only wasted our time and energy. Yes, you were wrong. There is no passage hidden behind this mirror. So listen to me now, both of you! We'd better go back to the main entrance and try to open it. No more stalling. Right now! Understood? Now!'

Chiara was right, thought Travis. *The guy is a real pain in the ass.* He held his gaze for a few seconds, then without another word or reaction to Randy's outburst, he turned and started to pace the chamber.

What now? Their situation was hopeless. He could feel the frustration boiling up inside him. Anger heated his blood and coiled in his stomach. He kicked his rucksack and, raking both hands through his hair, swore under his breath.

Chiara stood motionless, the fear growing in her eyes. Then, fists raised, eyes flashing anger, she began to pound on the mirror. 'I don't want to die. I want to get out of here. I can't stand …' Her voice trailed off. She stiffened.

Travis shot her a startled glance. 'What's the matter? What is it?'

She held up her hand to silence him. She

pounded on the mirror again in several different places and, pressing her ear against its smooth, glossy surface, listened.

His head tilted to one side, Travis stood, watching her.

She stopped pounding and straightened up. 'It looks like you were right after all. I think there is a hidden passage behind the mirror. Or at least an empty space. Listen to this sound.' She knocked a few more times on the mirror and on the adjacent wall. 'Can you hear the difference? Here, it sounds dull and hollow. But there …'

Randy, who had calmed down a bit, pushed his hair back from his forehead. 'But how are we going to reach this secret passage? Assuming of course that it's there. There seems to be no access. We've already looked everywhere and haven't found anything.'

'We must find a way to open it. It may be our only option for survival.' Travis's voice was filled with determination.

'Yes, but how?'

'This should do the trick,' Travis pulled his gun out of the holster.

'But you shouldn't destroy—'
He didn't let Chiara finish. 'We've got no choice.' And before she had time to react, he fired the gun three times, then took a quick step backwards.

CHAPTER 13

The snake-framed mirror shattered, and the cracking sound rebounded off the cave walls. Thousands of glittering black shards fell to the floor. A waft of damp, musty air rushed out. Travis stared at the dark gaping hole that had appeared where the smoky obsidian glass had been just a few moments ago.

Randy was first to react. He moved closer and, shining the torch in, looked inside. Travis walked up behind him and peered over his shoulder. A circular tunnel stretched ahead of them. Water trickled down the ragged walls. The gently sloping floor was uneven and littered with gravel and pieces of broken rock.

Relief spread over Travis like a warm blanket. It looked like they had found the secret passage, at last! But doubts crowded his mind. Where did it lead to? What if it was just another dead end?

'I'll go in first. Give me the light,' he demanded.

'Why you?'

'Just give me the light.'

The volcanic glass shards crunching under his feet, he squeezed through the small opening, careful not to cut himself on the sharp edges, and stepped into the roughly hewn passageway. Before venturing any deeper, he motioned for Chiara and Randy to follow him.

'What are you waiting for. We have to see where it goes. Come on,' he urged them, and advanced with caution, waving the torch beam around to illuminate the craggy floor and walls.

They inched their way down the dank-smelling tunnel in silence. In the ominous stillness, Travis could hear the steady *plink* ... *plink* ... *plink* of dripping water. The further they went, the stronger it grew, until it drowned out the ragged breathing and the thudding of his own heart. The humidity spiked, and the air became even more thick and cloying than before.

Just then, a new sound intruded upon his senses, faint but distinguishable. A fluttering of wings. Startled, Travis stopped and listened, trying to determine where it came from. Suddenly, a blur of movement caught his eye. He looked up. Several bats flew right above his head, and with a high-pitched squeak, disappeared into the darkness.

'That's a good sign. They must have an exit point somewhere close by,' remarked Chiara.

'Well I hope it's big enough for us to pass through.'

The straight passageway ended with a short flight of steps, which took them to a wide corridor filled entirely with water. An underground river. Travis stopped on the bottom step, and tried to see what lay beyond. On one side, a rock outcropping blocked his view. On the other, he saw what looked like a narrow archway. He nodded towards it. 'There seems to be something over there. An opening. But I can't see what's on the other side, so I'm not sure which way we should go.'

'Let's try the one with the narrow passage,' suggested Randy.

Chiara descended one step, stopping right behind him, so close that he could feel her warm breath on his neck.

'You both better wait here. I'll go in first to see where it leads,' she said.

'No. Too risky. What if you get lost? We'd better stick together,' Travis protested, and turned towards Randy. 'Will you be able to swim with your injured leg and arm?'

'It won't be easy, but I'll have to do it if it's the only way to get out of here. I have no choice, do I?'

Chiara was the first to lower herself into the

water. She heaved a sigh of relief. 'It's not as deep as I thought it would be,' she told them.

Travis was next. Holding the rucksack and torch high in the air, he slowly slid into the turquoise water. He sucked in a breath at the first contact. It felt as though thousands of tiny needles were pricking his skin. The water was cold. Icy cold. He hadn't expected that.

Ignoring the discomfort, he waded through the water towards the arched, narrow passage. A loud splash told him that Randy, too, was now in the water.

'Watch out! The water gets deeper here. I've lost my footing, I'll have to swim now,' called Chiara from inside the narrow passage.

Travis waited for Randy to catch up with him. 'I can't swim with the light. I'll have to switch it off. So you go first, I'll follow behind.'

Randy shook his head. 'Don't switch it off too soon. Wait until I get over there.' He pointed to the arched opening and began to wade towards it. Halfway there, he turned and, as if sensing Travis's impatience, added, 'I can't move any faster. The injuries slow me down.'

Travis clenched his teeth against the icy chill seeping into his bones, numbing his limbs, and waited. As soon as Randy had disappeared inside the arched opening, he switched off the torch and put it in the backpack. The pitch black surrounded him and he couldn't see anything. Now he had but his memory of the place and his sense of hearing to guide him. Gathering all of his strength, he thrust his body forward in long strokes. He entered the narrow passage and kept swimming. He could hear the gentle splashing of Chiara and Randy not too far away.

'The water is shallow here. I can walk now,' Chiara called out.

Travis pushed his feet hard and almost immediately felt them touch the bottom. Head and shoulders above the surface, he moved forward slowly. The further he got, the shallower the water became. When it was down to his waist, he stopped and pulled out his torch again. Slowly, he flashed on the beam and, squinting at the sudden brightness, took in his surroundings.

Irregular, cracked and pitted limestone walls in various shades of earth tones, ranging from warm brown through soft sandy to the palest of grey, rose on both sides of the jade-green body of water. Countless mica-studded stalactites were hanging right above his head, sparkling in the torchlight like splendid diamond chandeliers.

'Wonderful. This place looks almost magical. Under different circumstances I would enjoy being here,' said Chiara, glancing around.

'Yeah, it looks really amazing,' agreed Randy, moving closer to her. 'I've never seen anything like this before.'

'But I've got no idea where we are, or where the exit might be. I've never been in this part of the underground before. I hope we're moving in the right direction.' She shook her head in dismay.

They continued to follow the river as it wound its way around the rock formations. It widened, turning into a subterranean lake that filled a vast but rather low-ceilinged cavern almost entirely. Eager to grab at the chance to get out of the icy cold water, they swam across it towards the rocky shore and, shoes squelching, inched their way along the slippery shoreline, scrutinizing every nook and cranny in search of an exit.

Chiara sighed. 'There's nothing here. We'll have to go back to the water, find where the river flows out of the cave and follow it.'

Travis wasn't ready to give up yet. 'Wait, I'll check what's behind that large boulder over there.'

He rounded the boulder and saw a crevice wide enough for a man to pass through with ease. Parts of the stone around the edges were blackened, as if by smoke and soot from burning torches. In one corner stood two ceramic pots and two clay figurines, all covered with a thick layer of limestone dust.

'I found something,' he called out. 'I guess it's the entrance to a passage. It seems to have been used by the Maya centuries ago. Come on, let's see where it leads. Who knows, it may take us to an exit.'

One by one, they entered the crevice and soon found themselves in a rather small, rectangular space where the roof had the shape of a corbel arch, and two tunnels branched off in different directions. A red stone, life-size head wearing an animal mask, tongue and eyeballs protruding in a menacing manner, lay on the ground. Three ceramic pots stood beside it, the once bright red, black and yellow colours they were painted with now tarnished and faded. Curious as to what they contained, Travis glanced inside. All he saw were ashes.

'What are these? Funeral urns?' he asked.

'Could be. This place looks like a burial vault to me.' Randy paced the floor nervously.

'Where should we go now?' Chiara leaned her head sideways and squeezed water out of her hair. Her wet clothes were clinging to her body, revealing the curves of her shapely figure. Travis couldn't stop his gaze from drifting towards it.

The corners of her mouth twitched as she caught his stare. 'Where should we go now?' she repeated, with a distinct note of impatience, her fingers raking through the long, silky strands of dark blonde hair. 'Stop gawking at me.' She shifted her gaze towards Randy. 'Both of you. Tell me which way we should go.'

Randy shrugged. 'How should I know?'

Travis inspected the stones around both tunnel entrances, but found nothing to help him decide. He straightened up. 'I have no idea. I'm not sure whether we should enter either of these tunnels. Maybe we've got a better chance of getting out if we follow the river.'

Chiara gave him a disapproving look. 'I don't think so.' She peered into both gloomy openings. 'Well, I see neither of you can decide, so I'll have to. And I've got nothing but my instincts to guide me.' She paused, then pointed to the tunnel on her left. 'Let's try this one.' She gestured for them to follow her.

Travis decided not to waste time arguing, and stepped into the tunnel she had indicated. His shadow on the stone wall made him look like a giant. At first, he advanced with calm, cautious steps, eyes straining to pierce the darkness beyond. Then, seeing no obstacles, he quickened his pace. The tunnel twisted, turned and branched off in different directions.

It seemed to him as if they had been walking for a long time but in fact it might just have been a few minutes when he thought he heard something. He tensed, motioning for Chiara and Randy to be quiet. All three of them froze, listening. A distant murmur reached his ears. Voices. He could hear voices, and they were getting louder. Closer.

'Someone's coming. What if it's those thugs that attacked you? They mustn't see us,' he whispered.

'Quick! We have to hide somewhere.'

'Yeah, but where?'

'Switch off the torch.'

'Not yet. We need to find a hiding place first.'

Frantic now, his eyes darting around, Travis swiftly rounded a bend and saw the tunnel widen into a cavern. Several huge rock formations rose from the cave floor. Without thinking, he moved towards the nearest one.

The voices were becoming more distinct, getting closer and closer.

He switched off the torch. Darkness enveloped them. Feeling their way, and trying to make as little noise as possible, they took cover behind the craggy rocks. Just then, bobbing lights appeared in the far corner of the vast chamber, and heavy footsteps resounded on the stone floor. The lights grew brighter and brighter, the voices louder and louder, until they were loud enough for him to make out isolated words. They were speaking in Spanish.

It was too late to hide somewhere else. He could only pray that they wouldn't be discovered. He pressed his body to the rough stone, hardly daring to breath, while his fingers tightened their grip on the gun, ready to pull the trigger if the need arose. He wouldn't give in without a fight.

The footsteps were very close now. He could hear the squeak of the rubber boot soles on stone. A few moments later, some figures emerged out of the shadows. It was a large group of men.

He tilted his head to get a better look at the two men walking ahead of the others. One was rather short, sinewy, his face rough-hewn and weather-beaten, his mouth set into a hard line. The second one was a *mestizo*, medium height and slender but strong built, somewhere in his late thirties or early forties. There was something threatening about him. His large, deep-set eyes had a fiery intensity in their gaze and his angular face twisted into a predatory scowl as he talked. From his overbearing demeanour and the way he was dressed, Travis concluded he must be the boss. He shifted his gaze towards the rest of the group. He could make out several heavily armed men who were prodding some other men with their rifles and guns.

They advanced deeper into the cavern, then turned right and disappeared out of view. Their footsteps and voices faded away into silence.

Travis waited, not yet daring to move.

'That was them,' he heard Chiara whisper, her warm breath feathering his ear.

'You mean those brutes who attacked you?'

She nodded. 'Yes. And they've got my colleagues.' Her voice quivered with rage. 'What are they going to do to them? Where are they taking them? We have to find out. We have to rescue them.'

'No way! We'll only put ourselves in danger,' protested Randy. 'Have you seen how many of them there were, and the weapons they carried? We're no match for them. All we have are two small pistols. Two small pistols! You got it? So we'd better get out of here as soon as we can, and go and look for help.'

'Look for help? Where? We're in the middle of the jungle. It would be days before we got back with some help. They'll be long dead. Time is of the essence here, we have to act now. We have to find a way to save them. I can't just run away, I have to do something, try to free them.' Chiara's voice had risen, resonating with fierce determination.

'It's crazy to do that. It's too dangerous.'

'I *have* to try to free them. It's no use arguing with me. I won't change my mind.'

'Fine. What about you, Travis?' he asked.

'I agree with Chiara. We should try to save them. They'll die if we don't.'

Randy took a sharp intake of breath. The irritation clear in his voice, he said, 'You know what, Travis? You really disappoint me. I thought you were more reasonable. Smarter. But I see I was wrong. You keep taking senseless risks, just like her. Yes, you are two of a kind. Don't you realise you're putting all our lives in danger? Did you see those men? Did you see how many guns they had? So why won't you listen to reason and try to get out of here while you can?'

Travis clenched his jaw, fighting the anger he felt at Randy's insolence. He slowly stood up from his crouching position, and switched on the torch. He swung the beam to his right. 'I saw them head this way. I think it's safe to go now. Come on, we have to find out where they are holding your colleagues. But be careful to make as little noise as possible.'

He took three cautious steps and froze, feeling a gun barrel press into the small of his back.

Randy breathed on his neck. 'No, we won't follow them. We'll go in the opposite direction, the one they came from.' He paused, heaved a deep sigh, then added, 'And no hard feelings. I had to do what I did. You just left me no choice. I don't want to get killed. I want to go home. See my son, keep my promise. He's waiting for me. He'll be sad if I don't come home. Don't you care?'

Travis cast a furtive glance over his shoulder. 'You're bluffing. You wouldn't dare shoot me.'

Randy smirked. 'I wouldn't be so sure if I were you.' He turned towards Chiara. 'Come here, closer, so that I can see you. And don't try anything. Otherwise I'll shoot him. I swear.'

It seemed his firmly spoken words and the look of wild determination flashing across his face were enough to convince her that he really meant what he said. She moved forward without trying to argue with him.

Once again, Randy poked him with the gun. 'So what are you waiting for? Move. Let's go.'

Obeying his orders, Travis took a couple of small steps in the opposite direction and then paused, stalling for time. 'Listen …'

Randy shoved the gun harder. 'Move! Don't stop. And keep quiet.'

Travis wasn't going to give up easily. He had to find a way to make Randy change his mind, or try to overpower him. His eyes darting around, his mind racing, he searched for something that would help. He took another step. 'You know those men will die if we don't rescue them. We should at least try. Those thugs don't even know about us. We could sneak up on them and—'

'Shut up!' Randy barked.

Undeterred, Travis continued, 'My younger sister, an archaeology student, came to Guatemala two years ago because she was fascinated by the ancient Maya culture—'

'Your sister? What she has to do with—'

'Just let me finish. She disappeared. That's why I came here, to Guatemala. To look for her. I've checked all the places she went to but I still haven't found her … I believe she's dead. Well, what I want to make clear to you is that I want to rescue those men … because it would feel somehow … I don't know … as if I was helping her.' He fell silent. His throat tightened at the thought of his sister.

'Sorry to hear about your sister,' said Chiara.

The pressure on his back slackened.

He turned around slowly and saw that Randy had lowered the gun. He stood, hands dropped to his sides, shoulders slumped. 'She disappeared in the jungle?' He asked and averted his gaze.

'Yes. I've found some evidence. Not enough. Got a few suspects and followed them.'

'Those guys we saw in Flores?'

'Yes. Guess I got too close.'

'They clearly didn't like it?'

'No, they didn't. Tried to scare me off.'

Randy scratched his ear. 'Okay, maybe you two are right. Maybe we should try to save them. Who knows, we might be able to help without being discovered by those ruthless thugs. And I'll have an interesting story to write about later. I could write a series of articles. Or even a book. But promise me you won't take any stupid risks.'

Chiara took a step towards him. 'Give me the gun. I'll feel safer if I carry it.'

'Do you know how to use it?' he asked, before handing it to her.

She rolled her eyes in disdain and snatched the gun from his hand. 'Let's go. We have to hurry. We don't know what those brutes are going to do. Maybe they're planning to kill them all. I'm afraid we'll be too late.'

CHAPTER 14

The thugs, who were more numerous and heavily armed than before, caught them all with ease. They were too weak and exhausted to struggle and, besides, they were cornered and had nowhere to run.

And now, as he shuffled down the gloomy and twisting tunnel, Greg wondered where they were taking them and what they were going to do to them. Tie them up and leave them somewhere again? Or maybe first torture, then kill?

He staggered when a squint-eyed, tobacco-chewing brute of sturdy build prodded him in the back with the barrel of his firearm, barking at him to move faster. Not wishing to provoke him further, he quickly regained his balance and lengthened his stride.

The tunnel turned, then branched off. They continued forward, following a narrow passageway that soon widened into a vast cavern. The two men walking ahead stopped as soon as they entered it.

Squinting against the bright torchlight, Greg took in his surroundings. His gaze swept over the obsidian mirrors adorning the walls, the broad staircase leading up to a rectangular platform with a sacrificial altar, and the imposing red-walled temple with two colossal, intricately carved jade statues flanking its entrance. A ritual chamber. A sacred place for the ancient Maya. From what he could see at a glance, this was a place where they would have held secret, black magic rites and bloodletting ceremonies.

It also looked somehow familiar. He realized he had been here before, shortly after the thugs had caught him the first time. He knitted his brow in concentration, trying to recall the route they had taken that time, but all he managed to extract from his memory was that they had meandered for quite some time through a tangled maze of tunnels and chambers, taking so many twists and turns that he had quickly lost track. He didn't know what section of the underground the ceremonial cavern was in, nor where the exit was. He feared it wouldn't be easy to get out of there, supposing they get the chance to try.

Why had they brought them to this place now? What did they want from them? To show them how to open the temple and help them find some hidden treasures? Would they kill them once they were done with them?

One of the villains – the one who seemed to be the leader – moved closer. The torchlight cast shadows on his face, accentuating his chiselled jawline and day-old stubble. He stopped in front of the prisoners and, smoothing a palm over his raven-black, slicked-back hair, swept his gaze over the defenceless men. His attention focused on Greg. He studied him with the intensity of a hunter, like he was prey. From under full, strong brows, his reptilian eyes glowed like molten amber, blazing with ill-suppressed fury and hostility.

Feeling uneasy under such ferocious scrutiny, Greg shrank back against the wall. A chill crawled down his spine. Something so cruel, so profoundly evil emanated from the man standing in front of him that it made him appear almost unhuman.

The snake-eyed man, as he began to call him, turned towards an older but strong and tough-looking guy. 'Tie them up. And make sure they can't escape this time. Don't let them out of your sight, even for a second. Understood?'

Greg cleared his throat. 'What do you want from us? Why won't you let us go? We are no threat to you. We haven't—'

'Shut up! You'll find out soon enough what I need you for.' With that, he jabbed both hands in his trouser pockets, spun on his heels and walked away. After just a few steps, he stopped and, turning once more towards the older, tough-looking man, said, 'The woman. The one who can read the ancient inscriptions. In all the commotion I almost forgot about her! You'd better go and check she hasn't got away. I'll stay here and watch over this lot with Fabio, Arturo and Jairo. You take the others and go, check on her. Do it now.'

'And what should I do with her? Leave her where she is, or bring her with me?'

'Bring her here. We'll let her enjoy the show. It will be more fun. And she might become more cooperative when she sees what treats we have in store for her companions.' He chuckled, rubbing his chin.

Greg had a sinking feeling in the pit of his stomach. Just as he feared, they were going to be tortured, and there was no hope of escape. And they'd caught Chiara as well. That meant they had caught all of them, and there was no one to alert the authorities. No one to come to their rescue. They could only rely on their own strength. And it was clear they were no match for these heavily armed thugs. He clenched his jaw with futile anger until his teeth began to ache. He tried but couldn't think of anything he could do to save himself and his colleagues. He shot a furtive glance at them. They looked defeated and lost, strain showing on their faces.

Once they'd been tied up again, Greg and his colleagues sat huddled at the far corner of the room, feeling the tension mounting with every minute that passed.

When the four men who had left to check on Chiara returned, it was clear from the expressions on their faces that they weren't bringing good news for the snake-eyed man.

'Why are you empty handed? I told you to bring her. Where is she?'

'We couldn't find her, she got away,' the older, rugged man said, his voice subdued.

'Couldn't find her?! You mustn't have looked properly.'

'We did, but she's definitely gone. I don't know how, but somehow she managed to break the ties. And she couldn't... I mean not alone... it would only really be possible if someone helped her ...'

'What?! You mean you didn't catch all of them? More of them got away?'

'No, we did catch them all. I'm sure of that. I just don't see how she could have done it alone. The ropes we tied her with were so strong, so thick. They'd be impossible to break. And yet there they lay on the ground, broken. I searched everywhere, but there was no trace of her. I'll go back to look for her, if you want me to. And I promise, I won't stop until I find her.'

The snake-eyed man glanced at his watch. 'No, don't go now, it's too late. We shouldn't waste any more time searching for her. I need you here. We have to get everything ready for the ceremony. Tonight is a full moon. It's the perfect time and we can't miss it. We'll look for her later. If she is still in the underground, we'll find her. And if she did manage to get out, then she won't get far in the jungle. Soon the night will fall.'

They stuck burning wood torches into the ceramic holders along the walls and the stairs leading to the red temple. The mellow golden light transformed the spacious cavern, giving it a spooky, somewhat magical appearance, enhanced by the countless black volcanic glass shards embedded in the reddish-brown rocks, twinkling like stars in the night sky.

Two of the men, guns in hand, stayed to watch Greg and his companions while the others were busy preparing for the 'ceremony', as the snake-eyed man had called it. Greg followed them with his eyes, trying to figure out what they were doing, but the flickering flames cast dancing shadows across the cave floor and walls, making it difficult to focus and distorting the visual perception of what was happening.

He frantically racked his brain to think of a way to escape, but he couldn't think of anything. He feared the thugs would kill them at the slightest attempt to escape, just as they had killed Juan earlier.

'What are they going to do to us?' Greg heard Daniel whisper, his voice full of anxiety. He was sitting slumped against the wall next to Greg.

'I don't know.'

'What ceremony are they talking about?'

'I'm not sure, I can't see what they—'

Before he had time to say another word, one of the two armed guards pushed him with the handle of his gun, and barked, 'Shut up!'

'No need to shout. I just—'

'Shut up!' he repeated, and hit him with the butt of the pistol, sending him sprawling against the wall.

Time passed. He had no idea how much. Maybe minutes. Maybe even hours. With the last hope for escape gone, he sat motionless, staring ahead at nothing in particular. He wondered when he had last eaten. A long time ago. But his mounting anxiety drowned out his hunger. His brain felt fuzzy and he couldn't think.

The snake-eyed man left the chamber, and when he reappeared Greg gasped. The man looked so different that he hardly recognized him at first.

The snake-eyed man had transformed into an otherworldly apparition. His entire face was painted bright azure blue. The Maya blue. The colour of Chaac, the rain god, and of human sacrifice. Elaborate jade earrings dangled from his earlobes. A large headdress adorned his head, made for the most part of scarlet macaw and iridescent green tail quetzal feathers. From its centre, a black snake reared in a fierce stance. A heavy necklace encircled his neck, composed of seven strands of jade and turquoise tube beads. On his chest hung a large jade pendant in the form of a human head. A deity mask. Around his waist was wrapped a beautifully decorated loincloth. The belt holding it was festooned with obsidian, fire opal and jade plaques. A cape of jaguar skin was draped over his shoulders. With every movement, his wrists and ankles clunked with bracelets made of carved shells and what looked like jaguar teeth and claws.

The look of pure astonishment on Greg's face seemed to amuse the snake-eyed man. He grinned, baring his gleaming white teeth menacingly.

On seeing the unexpected apparition, Greg's fear disappeared momentarily. His initial thought was: *Wow! That's exactly what an ancient Maya high priest must have looked like when he was about to take part in an important ceremony. What a wonderful rendition.* He felt as though he had travelled back in time. If the circumstances had been different and he wasn't being held captive, he would have looked forward to such an extraordinary performance. But, of course, what he was about to witness wasn't for his entertainment.

'Why is he dressed like that? Is he crazy?' he heard Antoine whisper.

The snake-eyed man was heading for the staircase leading up to the red temple on the opposite side of the room.

'What's going on? What kind of ceremony are they preparing for?' asked Daniel. Before Greg had time to answer, some of the men approached them.

'Untie them and strip off their shirts,' the older, tough-looking man ordered. He too was dressed like an ancient Maya. His costume was, however, much less splendid than the one his boss was wearing.

Once all of the prisoners were stripped to the waist, their exposed skin was covered with blue paint, the same bright azure colour of the snake-eyed man's face.

'Why are you doing this to us? What do you want?' Daniel said, gesturing wildly.

The tobacco-chewing guy pushed him with the butt of the gun. Hard. Daniel staggered, lost his footing and lay sprawled on the ground. The brute scowled and prodded him with his boot. 'Stand up! And be quiet. I'm warning you, next time I won't be so gentle.'

Daniel clambered slowly to his feet. Too slowly for the squint-eyed brute's liking, as he was prodded in the back and told to hurry. When he'd managed to stand up, he leaned his back against the wall and stood, watching his captors in silence, shoulders hunched, lips pressed together in a narrow line, eyes gleaming with repressed anger.

Greg lifted his head and looked at the older, tough-looking man. 'Listen, if you want us to tell you where the treasure is—'

'Treasure?' the old rogue interrupted him, smirking. His bronzed, rough-hewn face glistened in the amber glow of the torches. 'Treasure? You think we caught you and brought here for *treasure*? You are wrong, totally, totally wrong.' He leaned closer, angry sparks flashing in his dark eyes. 'This is our land. And the land of our ancestors. Yes, our native land! And you, you've got no right coming here and doing what you want, taking whatever you fancy. Do you hear me? You have no right to plunder our ancestors' graves and desecrate their remains. No right to steal anything from this land. Not a thing. *Comprende?* Do you understand?'

The man's violent outburst startled Greg. He shrank back, speechless.

The thugs prodded them with the gun barrels towards the broad flight of stairs leading up to the red temple. Greg's unease grew as he mounted the steps. *What are they going to do to us next?* he thought. His heart began to hammer wildly in his chest and his breathing quickened in anticipation. Beads of sweat dotted his forehead.

He drew in a deep breath in an attempt to calm his nerves. A sweet and husky resinous smell of burning incense filled his nostrils. Before stepping onto the platform, he hesitated. A gun jabbed into his spine, forcing him forward. He took another step and glanced around. To his left stood two drums, and next to them were several red and black painted vases and bowls. In the four corners, he noticed elaborately crafted ceramic incense burners, each one sending white spirals of fragrant copal smoke into the air. On the stone altar lay a couple of glossy black obsidian knives with bone handles carved into the shape of a snake. And behind the sacrificial table stood the snake-eyed man, poised, ready to begin the ceremony.

With a jolt like an electric shock, Greg finally realized what the ceremony was going to be: a human sacrifice ritual. The supreme sacrifice of the ancient Maya. He had seen murals depicting scenes of the brutal bloodletting and heart extraction rites the Maya used to perform quite frequently. And there was no doubt in his mind as to who the victims were going to be this time.

As the awful truth dawned on him, an icy fear gripped him, sending shivers through his entire body. Images of the horrible death he knew awaited him flashed through his mind. And there was nothing he could do now. There was nowhere to run, there was no escape.

Two of the brutes started drumming a steady beat. It seemed that the ceremony had started.

'They're going to cut us open and rip out our hearts,' whispered Daniel.

Greg remained silent, not knowing what to say. *Is this really happening?* he asked himself. *Are they actually going to rip out our hearts? This is crazy! I don't want to die like that. It can't be real, it can't be!*

The steady beat of the drums built to a frenetic pace, and Greg's heart pounded right along with it.

Suddenly, out of the corner of his eye, he detected a sudden movement.

Daniel made a lunge for the altar. Taken by surprise, the thugs did nothing to stop him. Emboldened, he grabbed one of the obsidian knives lying on the stone slab and put its blade to a round-faced villain's throat.

The frenzied drumbeat stopped. Silence fell over the cavern. No one dared breath. All eyes were fixed on Daniel.

He swallowed, glaring at the gang leader. 'You let us go free. Now! Or—'

'Or what?' the snake-eyed man interrupted, fixing him with an unblinking stare. 'You'll kill him?' A guttural, sinister laugh burst from his mouth, echoing throughout the vast chamber. He pulled a gun from the belt wrapped around his loincloth and raised it. 'Do you really think that will stop me from killing you? What a fool you are. A complete fool. You shouldn't have done this, it wasn't a smart move. You have left me no choice now but to kill you both.'

Without hesitation, he fired two shots in quick succession.

Both Daniel and the round-faced thug fell to the ground.

It would be much better to die like that. Much less painful, Greg thought, and taking advantage of his guard's inattention, he dashed for the altar. Just before he reached it, someone grabbed him and held him tight. In a frenzy, he thrashed and kicked, trying to loosen the grip, but it was like an iron clasp. He kept wriggling and struggling, but no matter what he did, he couldn't shake the attackers off.

Suddenly, he felt a sharp blow to his head, and everything went black.

CHAPTER 15

The infernal din of drumbeats resounded in the air, drilling into his skull, reverberating in his ears. And then it stopped, as suddenly as it had started. An ominous and unsettling silence fell. A feeling of unease washed over Travis. Something wasn't right. He could sense it. His instincts told him something bad was about to happen. His skin prickled with anticipation, and he shifted into a more comfortable position. He listened, trying to detect the slightest sound.

Tense seconds ticked by. Nothing. He couldn't hear a thing.

Why is it so quiet? What are they doing in there? he wondered. The last question had hardly crossed his mind when a gunshot rang out.

Shortly after, another.

Travis, Chiara and Randy froze and held their breath.

What had happened? Were they warning shots? Was anyone wounded? Or even worse, killed?

The three of them were hiding behind a large boulder, backs pressed against a rough and cold rock wall. Only a faint amber glow coming from the vast chamber ahead thinned the dark gloom that surrounded them, as – afraid of being discovered – they had switched off their remaining torch.

They waited for the situation to evolve, not daring to move closer and peer inside the ritual cavern.

His right hand tight around his gun, eyes fixed on the dimly outlined entrance, Travis strained to pierce the foreboding silence that, after the gunshot echoes had faded away, once again enveloped the cave.

Long, tense seconds went by.

Then, the sound of a commotion reached his ears, amplified in the vastness of the cavern: heavy boots thumping, voices raised in alarm, a bone-wrenching scream, a throaty cackle.

'What's going on? What are they doing to them? I hope they haven't killed them,' whispered Chiara, shifting impatiently. 'We can't afford to wait any longer. We have to go in there now and see what's happening. See if we can do anything to stop it.'

'Now? Go in there now? You must be out of your mind! It would be an outright stupid thing to do. Can't you see it's too risky? We'll only put ourselves in danger,' protested Randy.

'Yeah, it's too dangerous to go in there now. We'd better wait,' agreed Travis.

'Wait? Wait for what?' Chiara snapped. 'We've been waiting for I don't know how long already. I've got no intention of standing here for hours, doing nothing. If we wait any longer, it may be too late to save them. We should act right now. Every minute counts.'

Randy sighed. 'Go, if you want to, I'll wait here. I won't take unnecessary risks. I told you, I've got a son waiting for me at home.'

Travis rubbed his forehead. 'Randy is right, we should wait until those thugs leave. It will be easier to free them then.'

'But what if they don't leave? What if they torture and kill them while we're standing right here, waiting for the perfect opportunity to present itself? What if this is the only chance we have to save them?' She swallowed, as if trying to force away the emotion clogging her throat. 'Besides, I don't mean we should attack them straight away. I'm not crazy. I realize we're not a match for them. But we do have one advantage over them: the element of surprise. They don't know we're here. Anyway, all I want to do is sneak in and size up the situation to see what they're up to and what we can do. You don't need to come if you don't want to. I can go alone.'

Travis grabbed her arm. 'Don't! It really would be better to wait a bit longer. You're taking too much risk. They'll catch you.'

She shrugged his hand away. 'Stop being so protective. I know what I'm doing. My mind is set – I'm going in there now. Alone, if I must. Give me your binoculars, I'll need them.'

Obediently, he handed her the binoculars. She put the strap around her neck. Then, as if regretting being so harsh, she leaned closer, patted his shoulder and whispered softly, 'Don't worry, I know how to move without attracting attention. I'll be as quiet as possible. I've seen what those brutes are capable of, how dangerous they are. Trust me, I'll be careful. Very careful. I want to save my colleagues, and I won't do that by getting killed.'

Chiara stepped out from behind the boulder and edged to the entrance.

'She's crazy,' muttered Randy. 'Totally nuts.'

Travis took a deep breath, then exhaled slowly. Why did he let her go alone? It was too dangerous. He shouldn't let her go by herself, it wasn't right. It wasn't in his nature not to try to help. He had to protect her.

He turned to Randy. 'I'm going with her. You coming?'

'No, I told you, I'm staying here.'

'Fine, as you wish. Don't do anything stupid. Wait for us here, we won't be long.'

Feeling his way along the wall, Travis moved in the direction of the pulsing glow of the torches until he saw Chiara emerge from the shadows. She stopped by the entrance. Then, flattening against the wall, she cautiously peered inside. She must have heard him approaching because she turned her head, and spoke in a hushed voice.

'We're lucky. No one's down here. They all seem to be up on the platform in front of the red temple. From what I can make out, that's where all the action's taking place. Next to the sacrificial altar.' She frowned. 'Something isn't right.'

'What makes you say that?'

'I don't know. I just have a feeling something isn't right, but I can't quite put my finger on it. They've lit so many torches. The whole chamber is ablaze with light. It makes me wonder what they are up to. I guess they brought them here with a purpose. I don't think they're going to just tie them up and leave them here like they did last time. They've got other plans now. I have to find out what those plans are.' She lifted the binoculars to her eyes and, leaning forward, looked inside the cave again, studying it in silence.

'I can't really see what's happening from here. I have to go inside.'

'Why you? I'll go. And if anything goes wrong, if they see me, don't waste a second. Just run away and hide.' He took a step forward.

She grabbed his shirt. 'Don't be so impulsive. There's no need to play the hero. Let me check what's going on in there. It's less risky. I know how to move inconspicuously and I'm smaller, so more difficult to spot.'

Travis hesitated, unsure what to do. The cavern was well-illuminated, but there were still some shadowy spots, enough for both of them to move about unnoticed. He lifted his head, fixing her with a steady gaze. 'We'll go together.'

'No. Stay here. I'd better go alone. Anyway, I won't be long.'

'Well, if you insist. But don't go too far. Promise you'll pull back at the slightest sign of danger.'

'I promise,' she whispered softly, eyes locked on his. 'Don't worry, I'll be careful.' She put her hand on his shoulder and gave it a gentle squeeze, then, with a stealthy step, advanced deeper into the vast cavern. She stayed in the shadows and, crouching low, moved with silent ease, slithering like a snake between the rock formations.

He stood still, leaning against the wall with his gun drawn. He followed her with his gaze, surprised at how nimble she was. To his relief, there seemed to be no imminent danger. All their enemies seemed to be up on the platform, occupied with what they were doing, seemingly unaware of their presence.

Chiara climbed a small rock outcropping from where she had a better view of the group of men gathered around the sacrificial altar without the risk of being discovered. The long stalactites drooping from above hid her slender figure from them, but allowed her to see what they were doing. She raised the binoculars to her eyes and peered through the lenses.

Travis released a breath he didn't even realize he had been holding, and straightened to relieve the ache in his shoulders. Chiara seemed to be managing all right. He turned his attention to the stone platform in front of the red temple. Several figures were moving around, but from his position it was impossible to make out their features or see what they were doing. He dared to inch a step closer and craned his neck to get a better view. One of the men seemed to be wearing an unusual costume with a large headdress made of colourful feathers. He blinked, unsure if he had seen what he believed he had seen, or whether he'd imagined it.

He hadn't imagined it, it was all real. The long, vividly coloured feathers of the man's headdress swayed as he moved, and the heavy-looking necklace on his bare chest reflected the torchlight, glittering.

Why is he dressed like that? Who is he? he wondered. *Chiara was right, they're up to something.*

The struggle appeared to be over. The men were less agitated now, their voices lower, hardly more than a murmur, interspersed with muffled moans. Despite his efforts, Travis couldn't see what was going on up there.

Eventually curiosity got the better of him and

he took one more step into the spacious chamber. Then another. The mellow light of the torches made the place look spooky. The air was rich with the sweet smell of incense and tinged with the metallic odour of blood. His earlier feeling of unease intensified. A chill of foreboding coursed through his body. A tingling sensation at the back of his neck warned him to be alert, and beads of perspiration dripped from his brow, stinging his left eye. He rubbed at it with his shirt cuff, then cast a wary glance around him to make sure no one was lurking in the shadows. The coast was clear. He flexed his fingers around the gun and, ignoring the pervasive sense of uneasiness, ventured deeper into the cave.

The drumbeat returned, even more frenzied than before.

A bloodcurdling scream ripped through the air, rising above all other sounds,

Travis stopped dead in his tracks.

He was about to move closer when the torches at the top of the stairs flared, sending sparks into the air. Were they going to come down? He took a step back and waited, eyes fixed on the stairway. It remained empty. He waited a little longer, then finally dared to take another step forward.

An electric torch was lying on the ground, not far from the staircase. He hesitated, wondering if he should take it. Their old one might die soon, and without light it would be very, very difficult, if not impossible, to get out of the underground. The problem was, the torch was lying in a well-lit area. To get it, he would have to leave the safety of the shadows. After some consideration, he decided it was worth a try. Crouching low, he made a dash for it. The sound of his blood pumping in his ears was so loud that, if not for the drumbeat, he was sure the thugs would be able to hear it. In one swift move, he picked up the torch, then quickly retraced his steps.

He was about to duck behind a stalagmite when he sensed someone moving right behind his back. Who was it? A surge of adrenaline shot through his veins, making his heart beat faster.

Too late to run away now, he thought. *I'll have to fight.* A muscle flickered in his jaw. His finger tightened on the trigger as he turned to see who it was.

'Hey, don't shoot. It's only me.' Chiara held up her hands. The light from the flickering torches cast an eerie orange glow on her sweat- and dust-streaked face, accentuating the look of cold dread that spread across it.

He lowered the gun. 'You scared me.'

'Come on, there's no time to lose.' She headed for the dark outline of the exit and motioned for him to follow.

Travis scampered behind her. They left the ritual cavern and entered the adjacent, smaller cave. Darkness surrounded them. They inched their way back towards their earlier hiding place, behind a huge boulder.

Apart from the muffled sound of the drumbeat, the low-roofed chamber was strangely quiet.

'Are you all right, Randy?' Travis whispered into the darkness.

There was no answer.

'Where is he?' asked Chiara, her voice anxious. 'Why is he so still? Maybe he collapsed from the injuries he sustained earlier. They were probably worse than we thought. We'll have to check, but we need light. Where have you put the torch?'

Leaning against the rough, jagged wall, Travis switched on the electric torch he had found in the ritual chamber and swept the beam around the cave.

It was empty. Randy was nowhere to be seen.

He saw his own backpack propped against the boulder. He picked it up, then switched off the light. Anger rose like bile in his throat and he felt his blood boil. He gritted his teeth, his fingers clenched around the backpack strap, nails digging into the padding. 'He's gone. What a bastard. What a selfish bastard!' To vent some of his annoyance, he kicked the gravel on the floor and swore under his breath.

'Calm down. Maybe he's waiting for us somewhere else.'

'No, he's gone. He decided to get out of the underground on his own. Thinks he's smart enough to find his way back. I had a bad feeling about him from the very start. My instincts told me not to trust him.'

'But he can't get far without a light.'

'He has light. He took my torch. I found this one in the ritual chamber. It's lucky I had the presence of mind to take it.'

'So he left, taking with him the only torch we had? Knowing we had no other light?'

'Yeah.'

'What a bastard!'

'That's what I said. A bastard. A real selfish bastard. We must find him.'

She grabbed his arm. 'No. We don't have time for that now. Let him go. Even if he finds the way out, he won't be able to get far in the jungle. We need to stay and try to save my colleagues. We have to act fast, otherwise those ruthless bandits will kill them.'

'Were you able to see what they were up to?'

'Yes, I was. And it's so horrible, you'd never guess. I could hardly believe my eyes…'

'Just tell me what you saw,' Travis said, unable to control his impatience.

She cleared her throat. 'Well, it looks as if they are about to perform some sort of a sinister ritual, like the ancient Maya used to do to appease their gods or angry spirits of their ancestors.'

He gasped. 'You mean a human sacrifice?'

'Yes. It looked like everything was set up ready to perform the ritual. They're going to kill them soon, probably by decapitation or heart extraction. What a horrible way to die.'

Travis shook his head. 'That's crazy. Human sacrifices? In this day and age? You must be kidding, why would they do something like that?'

'Don't ask me, I'm just telling you what I saw.'

'I find it hard to believe.'

'But it's true. There's no doubt about it in my mind. Everything I saw points to that. The altar, obsidian knives, incense burners, ceremonial pots, bodies painted in the Maya blue. And two of the thugs were wearing costumes, just like the ancient Maya would while performing human sacrifice rituals.'

'So it means they're going to kill them all. How awful! Such a horrible death. And there's no one else to save them but us. But what can we do? How can we stop them without putting ourselves in danger?'

'I don't know.'

'Did you see your colleagues? How were they?'

'Not good. They looked dazed, some didn't even move. I almost didn't recognize them at first because they've been stripped to the waist and painted blue. Their hands and feet are tied up so they can't fight. I saw blood, quite a lot of it splashed on the floor and the altar. So it might be too late to save some of them. We must act fast if we want to save the rest.'

'Yeah, but how do we do it without putting

ourselves in danger? It's only the two of us now.'

'I know, but we've got guns. That's something. The first time they attacked me, I didn't even have a gun to defend myself with.'

'Only two small guns though. Have you seen how heavily armed those thugs are? We don't stand a chance against them. They'll catch us and kill.'

'So we should use the element of surprise.'

'How?'

'I don't know, but we must do something before it's too late. They are going to kill them if we don't.' She sounded frantic. Almost hysterical.

He cupped his hand across his forehead, his mind racing. 'I'm well aware of that. And I'm considering the options. Not that we have many.'

'Hurry up. There must be something we can do.'

Travis drew a deep breath and massaged his temples, as though to knead clarity. It didn't help. Nothing but jumbled thoughts filled his brain. Panic began to gnaw at his determination.

'They'll kill them. We can't afford to wait any longer. We have to do something now!' Chiara whispered close to his ear. 'We can sneak inside, and try to shoot at them from a hiding position.'

'No, too dangerous. We wouldn't be able to escape.' He clasped his hands in front of his face. 'I can't think. I need to concentrate.'

All of a sudden, the drumbeat stopped. Once more, ominous silence enveloped them.

Travis straightened up. 'You've given me an idea. It's risky, but it might work. We won't know unless we try. There's nothing else I can think of. Come on.'

'What do you want to do? Where are we going?'

'I have to check something. I need to find out whether those caves are connected. If they are, my plan might work. Let's go!'

CHAPTER 16

The bone-chilling cold seeping into Greg's body forced him to open his eyes. He moved, wincing at the jarring pain that shot like a thunderbolt through his scalp and down his right side. He felt dazed and confused. Then he remembered the fight and the knock to his head that had made him lose consciousness.

How long had he been out? Seconds? Minutes? Hours?

In the eerie silence that enveloped the place, he could hear his own heart pounding like there was a wild animal trapped inside his chest.

Gradually, the haze lifted from his mind and questions began to storm it.

Why was it so quiet? What had happened to his colleagues? Were they all dead? Was he the only one left alive? Where were the snake-eyed man and the other thugs?

Squinting against the flickering torchlight, he looked around him but couldn't see much. Everything appeared blurry, his eyes unable to focus. Blood roared in his ears like the crashing of waves against rocks. An awful headache pounded his forehead. He tried to sit up, but it wasn't easy to lift his sore body with his wrists bound.

Finally, after a few clumsy attempts, he managed. He flexed his shoulders to ease some of the stiffness and was about to take another look around when the tough-looking, muscled brute standing close by shoved him back to the floor. Then, as if deciding it was not enough to punish him for his audacity, the sadistic bastard gave him a vicious kick in the ribs. Greg's half-naked body hit the floor with a thud. He clenched his teeth to stop himself from crying out at the sharp pain that seared through his left side. He didn't want to give him the satisfaction of knowing how much it hurt. To his relief, the agony was brief.

Once the pain had subsided, he lifted his head and looked around, his eyes straining to pierce the thick haze of copal incense hanging in the air. To his left, he could see three of his colleagues slumped on the floor, hands bound, faces contorted with a mixture of fear and powerless rage.

He could see some figures moving quietly

around the stone altar. In the smoky fog of incense shrouding them, they almost looked like ghostly apparitions performing a secret ritual.

What are they doing? he wondered, as he craned his neck trying to get a better view, though he still couldn't see much. It was only when one of the men moved aside that he saw that there was someone lying on the sacrificial table, motionless, blood dripping down his side onto the ground, creating a gory mess. He blinked, refusing to believe what he was seeing, refusing to believe that his ruthless captors had actually gone through with their horrific plans and performed the sinister ritual of human sacrifice. Part of him hoped that this wasn't really happening, that it was just a dream, a nightmare from which he would soon wake up.

He squeezed his eyes shut in an attempt to clear his vision. Yet, when he opened them a moment later, the sight hadn't changed. Aghast, he stared at the scene evolving in front of him. A cold chill crawled up his spine. It was not a dream. This was happening for real. Another of his colleagues had just been brutally murdered.

Are these crazy, bloodthirsty thugs going to murder all of us? he asked himself.

He remained rooted to the spot, not daring to move. Helplessness and frustration gripped him. He was unable to do anything except close his eyes to the horror around him and cling to a fleeting hope that his life would somehow be miraculously spared. Body tense, he waited for the thugs to choose their next victim, praying silently it would not be him, hoping for something to happen that would make them change their mind and stop the senseless killings.

Each agonizing second stretched like eternity. Nothing happened.

The five men standing around the altar didn't move. They appeared to be in a trance. He presumed they were communicating silently with the spirits of their ancestors or one of the sinister rulers of the underworld.

With each passing second, Greg's agony and desperation increased. He started to wish for an end to the ordeal as soon as possible, no matter what that entailed.

Suddenly, a shot rang out, cutting through the thick silence like the sharp obsidian blade the snake-eyed man was holding in his outstretched hand. The bullet ricocheted off the wall, echoing across the cave.

It took Greg a moment to understand what had just happened. Someone else must be there in the cavern. But who? Who had fired the gun? Was it Chiara? If so, was she alone or had she brought help? A surge of hope swept through him. He held his breath in anticipation.

The men gathered by the altar looked stunned. They stared at each other with confused looks on their faces. The other thugs also appeared baffled. It was clear from the expression twisting their features that the gunshot was not part of the ritual. Someone seemed to have thwarted their gruesome plans. Greg could hardly stop himself from smiling.

The thugs stirred, emerging from their initial stupor. They drew their guns.

'Someone else is in the room,' muttered the leader of the gang, his eyes darting around the chamber. 'What are you waiting for? Go and find him, now! Don't let him get away.'

'It might be the woman,' said the guy with the bodybuilder physique.

'No, it can't be her. She had no gun. I checked before I tied her up. And I'm sure there was nowhere she could get hold of one,' the older man disagreed.

'Whoever it is we must get him. Hurry up! Come on!' urged the leader, while he removed the elaborate headdress he was carrying and put it down on the floor.

They had barely reached the top step when another shot rang out. The sound was muffled slightly, as if fired in an adjacent cave or tunnel. And then another one, coming from the opposite side of the underground.

The snake-eyed man spun around, eyes sweeping over the vast chamber. 'There is more than one shooter.'

'They sound like warning shots,' said the man with a thick moustache. 'Why have they fired warning shots?'

'I don't know. Could be to lure us out of the cave. Maybe they've set up a trap. So stay on your guard! Be careful where you step.' He pointed to a line of blazing flames, and lowered his voice. 'There's too much light here. Makes those remaining on the platform an easy target. Better snuff out some of those torches.'

The man with the weather-beaten face complied with his orders, extinguishing three of the four flambeaus. Then, brandishing their guns, the thugs descended the stairs. Greg could hear their soft footsteps and hushed voices as they scampered around the cavern. They were probably checking every nook and cranny.

Another burst of gunfire tore out. The sound of breaking glass followed, thousands of shards hitting the stone floor with a shrill tinkle.

Greg stiffened. He waited, unsure of what was going to happen next.

The last echoes faded away and silence fell. Abrupt and profound. All movement stopped downstairs.

Have they left the cavern? he wondered. *Have they found any of the shooters yet?*

He lay still, listening. All was quiet.

Greg darted a glance at both of the armed guards. They were pacing the floor with uneasy steps, heads turned the other way. In the semi-gloom surrounding the red temple, their rifle barrels glinted menacingly with each movement they made.

The torchlight flared, spitting sparks. Something else glinted on the floor. Straining, Greg made out an obsidian blade lying close to the stone altar.

I could use that as a weapon, he thought. *If only I could get hold of it without them noticing ... but how?* It seemed like an impossible task.

Should he take the gamble and go for it? It might be the last and only chance he had to try to regain his freedom. But what if the thugs find the shooters and kill them? No one else would come to save them and those crazy guys would kill him for sure, they'd rip his heart out. *If I have to die, then I'd prefer to die from a gunshot*, he thought.

He hesitated, unsure what to do, weighing up his options. He needed more than just a moment of the guards' inattention to grab the knife. Otherwise he risked being shot before he got to it. And he really didn't want to die. Finally he decided to proceed with caution and try to get rid of the ropes without the use of the obsidian blade.

For a while he squirmed against the bindings around his wrists, trying hard not to attract any attention. To his frustration, no matter what he did, the stout ropes just wouldn't loosen. With effort, he pushed himself to a sitting position. This time no one reacted to him doing so. Emboldened, he moved closer to one of the jade statues and examined it, searching for sharp edges.

Seeing the guards approach, he stopped what he was doing. The taller of the two shot him an angry glance and was about to say something when a hollow cracking sound rang out, as if someone had hit a rock with a stone. Reacting on instinct, guns at the ready, both men turned to look in the direction of the noise.

Greg gazed around, straining to see who else was in the cavern. He could see no one downstairs.

There was another cracking sound on the opposite side of the cave, followed by a dull thud, like the sound of a stone rolling. Step by cautious step, the guards advanced in different directions, their tense gazes searching the chamber, attempting to penetrate its farthest recesses.

Suddenly, out of the corner of his eye, Greg saw Antoine move. He turned to tell him not to try anything stupid, but before he had time to open his mouth the young man had rolled to his knees and began to creep towards the knife. Greg sat aghast, watching him as he manoeuvred the sharp blade between his bound wrists, the ropes falling to the ground.

A shot rang out, jolting him out of his stupor. One of the guards arched his back and toppled off the platform. Greg craned his neck, straining in the semi-gloom to see who had shot him. He could see no one downstairs. A split second later gunfire erupted, countless bullets ripping through the air. It was the second guard who was shooting, aiming, he assumed, in the direction from which the bullet that had killed his colleague had come.

Greg felt a hot rush of blood to his temples and the wild thumping of his heart. This was the moment he had been waiting for. The right moment to attack the enemy and try to escape their clutches. Kevin and Ramiro seemed to be thinking the same, because he saw them struggle to their feet. Knowing he had only seconds in which to act, he began to crawl towards the altar. But his body seemed to disobey his will. It moved slowly. Far too slowly. He feared he wouldn't make it, before the thugs came back and caught them.

Antoine saw him struggle and hurried over. He cut the ropes around his wrists and ankles. Then, clutching the obsidian blade, he lunged at the gunman. He was swift, but not swift enough. Before he had a chance to plunge the knife into the thug's chest, the brute turned around and squeezed the trigger.

Antoine's mouth opened in a silent scream of agony. His blood spurted out everywhere. The knife dropped, clattering on stone. The young man arched his back and fell to the ground, dead.

His heart pounding like a drum, Greg bolted for one of the blazing wooden torches. He snatched it from its bracket, took aim and threw it with all his might. Then he ducked behind the jade statue.

Another round of gunfire. Another body hit the stone floor.

He poked his head out from behind the giant sculpture. The furrow between his brows smoothed. The guard's shirt had caught fire and it spread fast, engulfing him. He looked like another blazing torch. He dropped to the ground and rolled in a mad frenzy in a futile attempt to extinguish the scorching flames, his anguished screams rebounding off the cave walls.

Greg grabbed the thug's gun and ran for the stairs as fast as he could. 'Come on, hurry up,' he called to Kevin who was now the only other survivor.

Frantically, they rushed down the stairs towards the exit. Only a few metres separated them from it when a figure emerged from the shadows, making Greg stop in his tracks. He raised the gun, finger curling around the trigger.

'Don't shoot, it's me.' Chiara stepped into the pool of quivering torchlight and tilted her head so that he could see her clearly.

He lowered his weapon. 'I thought it was one of the thugs.'

'What about the others?'

'Dead. They killed them.'

'Hurry up!' Kevin pushed past Greg. 'We must hide. They'll be here any moment.'

Chiara nodded. 'Yeah, let's go!'

Just as Greg was about to step out of the chamber, he heard the thud of heavy footsteps on the stone floor. Voices rumbled through the cavern, echoing off the walls. The thugs were coming back.

He willed his body to move faster and entered the semi-circular, spooky tunnel, hoping it would lead them to safety.

CHAPTER 17

They exited the claustrophobic, dank-smelling tunnel and emerged into another cave. Torch in hand, Chiara hurried across the uneven floor, which was littered with bones and countless pieces of broken pottery. Kevin followed her closely, then Greg, running as fast as he could. Agitated voices and the cracking sound of gunfire drifted out from the darkness behind them. Heavy boots thudded on the hard floor, echoing off the walls.

Greg slowed down, gasping for air. He had to bend almost double as the roof sloped lower and lower. Then, all of a sudden, it lifted, allowing him to straighten his back and walk upright again. Casting furtive glances around, he wondered why Chiara had chosen to head this way. He could see no other exit anywhere, and there was nowhere to hide. Maybe he shouldn't have followed her blindly. Maybe he should have trusted his own instincts and continued down the tunnel. But now, with the thugs at their heels, it was too late to change direction. All he could do was hope she knew what she was doing and where she was going.

Greg lengthened his stride, shortening the gap between himself and Kevin. The cavern widened. Ahead he saw what appeared to be a rugged limestone wall. It blocked any further passage. Chiara stopped and shone the torchlight across it.

Greg's eyes widened. Huge, dark shapes loomed out of the gloom. One by one, ghostly looking creatures emerged out of the shadows. He couldn't help but gape at the elaborately carved stone figures representing various Maya gods. Each piece was crafted with a precision he had rarely seen before, attesting to the advanced stonecutting skills of the ancient Maya. The sight was so captivating that it made him forget the impending danger for a moment. Questions stormed his mind. Why were there so many? And why were they there? What was this place used for? Was there something precious hidden behind the wall? A secret passage, a chamber, a royal treasure trove?

Chiara dropped to her knees in front of a large and weird looking creature representing Chaac, the rain god. She pressed something in the middle of it and the statue slid aside, revealing a dark, circular opening, hardly big enough to crawl through.

'Go inside, quick!' she whispered, gesturing for him and Kevin to enter the tunnel. 'I have to close the passage so I'll go in last.' Before Greg had time to react, she had switched off the torch. Darkness enveloped them, sheltering from unwanted eyes.

He could hear footsteps pounding the stone floor. Running. Harder and faster. Coming closer. He shot a glance over his shoulder and saw a faint sheen of light on the stretch of tunnel floor visible through the entrance to the cave. It grew brighter as he watched it.

A renewed sense of urgency gripped him. The thugs would get them if they didn't hurry. He squeezed his body through the opening and fending off his ever-present fear of confined spaces, began to crawl forward through the pitch blackness, scraping his head against the low roof in the process. Kevin followed him, then Chiara. He could hear the faint rustle of their clothes, then a grating sound when the stone statue slid back into place, sealing the entrance behind them. Shortly after, he heard voices coming from inside the cave they had just left. Angry voices. Heavy boots thumping the stone floor.

That was close, he thought. A second or two more and they would have caught them.

The further he crept, the fainter the voices

grew until at last they died away altogether. Silence fell, so deep that he could hear his own heartbeat.

The twisting tunnel was damp and airless, its walls wet due to moisture seeping through the porous limestone. In places, water dripped from the ceiling, large droplets falling onto his head. It annoyed him that he couldn't wipe them away. There was no way to go but forward, so he continued creeping until his knees hurt from constantly rubbing them against the rough surface of the floor.

'How far have we got to go?' he asked, lowering his voice to a whisper, although there was no danger of being overheard.

'We're more than halfway now,' answered Chiara.

'Where does this tunnel lead?'

'To one of the caves lying behind the ritual chamber. On the opposite side of it.'

The tunnel grew even smaller, forcing them to crawl on their bellies. Greg inched forward with caution, fearing he might get stuck.

After what seemed like a long time, but which was probably no more than a couple of minutes, his forehead bumped against something hard. He couldn't go any further, but nor could he turn around, as the passageway was so narrow that there was no space to do so.

He lifted a hand and reached into the darkness. His trembling fingers encountered a smooth surface that felt like a polished stone. A wall. They were trapped. Blood roared in his ears like a stormy sea. He squirmed, and asked in a low, strangled voice, 'What now? How do we get out of here?'

Chiara switched on the torch. 'Don't panic, there's a way out. It's not a solid wall, just another statue blocking the exit. There is a secret mechanism that moves it aside. Look to your left and you'll find it.'

Greg blinked, his eyes adjusting to the sudden light. Then he saw it. A small serpent's head.

'All you have to do is turn it.' She switched off the light again.

He did as he was told. There came a soft, almost inaudible grinding sound. Tentatively, he stretched out his right hand. Where the wall had been, there was now just air. Unsure of what was beyond that, he crept forward with great caution.

He felt gravel beneath him, and a change in the air that told him he was out of the tunnel. He breathed a long sigh of relief and scrambled to his feet. It felt so good to finally be able to straighten up. He rolled his shoulders and stretched his arms above his head, then leaned against the wall, waiting for Kevin and Chiara to join him.

He heard a soft whoosh of air behind his back. Before he even had time to think of what or who produced the sound, the cold steel of a gun barrel dug into his flesh. He tensed. Panic rose in his throat, constricting it. The thugs knew about the secret passage and had been waiting for them by the exit. He wanted to say something, to warn his companions, but no words came out of his mouth. He wanted to run, but he couldn't move his legs. A shiver ran down his spine as he imagined the horrible death awaiting him. Then, his fear flipped into anger. He gritted his teeth. This time he would not let them take him captive without a struggle. What did he have to lose? He fumbled with his gun, trying to cock it.

A hand grabbed his arm and a man's voice whispered close to his ear, 'Don't move. Keep quiet.'

He tried to wrest his arm free. The gun dug deeper into his flesh. The stranger's grip tightened. 'I said don't move! And keep quiet.'

'Everything all right, Travis?' asked Chiara.

'Yeah, it's safe to come out. The coast is clear.'

The mysterious stranger released his arm and lowered the gun. 'I'm sorry I pointed a gun at you, but I didn't want to take any risks,' he said in a soft tone.

'You know this guy, Chiara?' Greg mumbled, confused.

'Yeah. It's Travis who rescued me. He found me in the cave and cut the ropes. If it wasn't for—'

'How many managed to escape?' Travis asked, before she could finish.

'Just Kevin and Greg. All the others are dead.

Those brutes killed them.' Chiara's voice trembled slightly. She took a deep breath, then continued, 'The tunnel helped us gain some time, but we better hurry. We must get out of this place before they realize their mistake and come looking for us here.'

'I can't see a thing. I've no idea which way I should go,' muttered Kevin.

'Just keep moving to your right.'

Trying hard to make as little noise as possible, they began to inch their way along the wall in total darkness. Greg advanced slowly, struggling to keep his balance on the uneven, sloping floor.

'We're hardly making any progress. We need light, switch on the torch,' said Kevin.

'It's too risky. We're too close to the ceremonial chamber.'

They continued walking through the darkness. The cave they were crossing remained silent. The muscles in Greg's neck and shoulders began to relax. It looked like the thugs hadn't yet figured out where they were.

Suddenly, he felt a change in the air. It became heavier, denser, more oppressive. He realized they had exited the chamber and entered a tunnel so narrow that his shoulders touched both rugged walls. The tunnel twisted and turned, sloped down, levelled out, sloped down, then levelled out again. After a while he could no longer tell which direction they were heading.

As he took another step forward, he felt the

air move more freely around him. The tunnel had ended. He kept walking. The utter silence that surrounded him began to worry him. He wondered whether he had strayed off the path and found himself alone.

'Hey, are you guys there?' he asked. 'You're so quiet I can't hear you.'

To his relief, Kevin answered him almost instantly. 'Don't worry, we're still here.'

'If we continue following the wall blindly, we risk taking a wrong turn and we'll get lost.' Chiara's voice sounded hollow, the words lingered in the air. 'I need to see where we are. It should be safe now to use the torch.'

'Yeah, we are far enough away,' agreed Kevin.

Chiara pressed down the switch and a bright beam of light pierced the darkness, revealing a medium sized cave with banded reddish yellow limestone walls and a few strangely shaped rock formations. Broken gravel littered the sandy floor.

'Yeah, just as I thought.' Travis glanced around. 'We should continue straight on.' He pointed to the semi-circular opening looming up ahead of them.

Greg studied him for a while, wondering who this guy was, and how he happened to be there. He appeared to be in his late twenties or early thirties and looked fit and strong beneath his dishevelled, dirt-stained clothes. How did he know the underground so well?

After a short pause they continued walking.

Now, with the light on, Chiara set a brisk pace. Greg tried not to pant as he struggled to keep up with her. They strode down a straight, man-made tunnel with an arched ceiling. The tunnel widened, then branched off in two different directions.

Chiara stopped and, looking at Travis, asked, 'What now? Which one should we take? Left or right?'

'I don't know.' His eyes darted from one dark tunnel opening to another. Two deep lines formed between his brows. His forehead was glistening with sweat and he rubbed it nervously. 'I'm not sure which is the right direction.'

'Don't you have a compass?' Chiara pushed back her hair.

'Yeah, I do, I forgot all about it in the commotion.' Travis rummaged in his backpack, then said through clenched teeth, 'It's not there. Randy must have taken it, the bastard!' He hesitated, then pointed to his left. 'Okay, let's go this way.'

Greg had lost all sense of direction by now, so he had no idea which way was the right way. He was too tired and too confused to think.

Moving as silently as they could, they entered another tunnel, which soon widened into a cave.

Another tunnel. Another cave. And another tunnel, long and winding like a snake. Then, again, another cave, until Greg lost count of how many tunnels and caves they'd passed through.

They finally emerged into a chamber with two walls painted bright red and two covered with multi-coloured murals. 'An impressive chamber,' said Chiara. 'I would have remembered it if I'd seen it before, but I don't. I've no idea where we are.'

Travis shook his head. 'Looks like we took the wrong turn.'

Greg sighed. 'So we must go back and try the other one.'

'Wait a moment.' Kevin stared at the colourful figures painted on the wall. 'This place looks familiar to me … I've seen those murals.' He paused, then smacked his forehead. 'Yeah, I know now. I've been here once with Antoine. If I'm not mistaken, there's a passage over there.' He rounded a large boulder. 'Yeah, it's here, just as I thought. From what I can remember, we're not far from the main exit, only about …' His voice trailed off. His body stiffened.

'What's wrong?' asked Greg.

'I thought I heard footsteps,' he whispered.

'What?'

'It sounded like someone walking stealthily.'

'They found us. And they are trying to sneak up on us.'

'Quick! We have to hide.'

'Shh!'

Greg ducked behind one of the rock formations a split second before Chiara switched off the torch.

THIRST OF THE RAIN GOD

CHAPTER 18

Squeezed between the wall and the stalagmite, Greg froze to listen, straining for the slightest sound. But there was nothing.

Kevin must have imagined it, he thought. He shifted his weight to ease the cramped muscles in his left leg and wiped his forehead with the back of his hand. The skin felt slick and sticky. Was it blood? Was there an open wound he didn't know about? Then he remembered the blue paint he'd been smeared with. That must be it. He rubbed his hand against his trousers to get rid of the pasty substance.

Just then the soft sound of footsteps reached his ears. So Kevin was right after all, someone was there. Who was it? He tried to see through the surrounding darkness, but it was too thick and he quickly gave up. He tightened his grip on the gun and held his breath in tense anticipation.

A dull thud resounded, as if something soft had knocked against hard stone. A muffled curse followed.

Chiara, who was crouching close to him, stirred. A bright beam pierced the darkness. Squinting against the light of Chiara's torch, he grabbed her arm and, squeezing it hard, hissed, 'Have you gone mad? What are you doing? Switch it off.'

'Calm down. There's no danger. I know who it is, I recognize the voice.' She wriggled her arm free and stepped out from behind the rocks. She walked up to the entrance of the tunnel and shined her light into it.

Travis strode over and peered inside. 'Well, well, what a surprise. Look who we have here! If it isn't our old friend the reporter. Safe and sound, but looking strangely lost. What happened? Why are you still in the underground? Can't find the exit? Don't know which way to go?' He sneered. Then, after he'd taken a deep breath, he continued, his voice dripping with hatred, 'So we meet again! You didn't think we would, did you? You didn't expect us to get out of there alive. But as you can see, we did.'

A tall man emerged from the tunnel, glassy-eyed and pale, his clothes torn, dirty and blood-stained. He held up his hands. 'Okay, okay, you have every right to be angry. I admit what I did was wrong. But you left me no choice. I tried to warn you, but you wouldn't listen.'

'You took the only light we had and left us for dead,' interrupted Chiara, her voice tight with resentment. 'How could you do that to us? You didn't care what would happen to us. You didn't give a damn whether we lived or died. All you cared about was saving your own ass.'

'Yeah, and you stole my compass,' Travis added.

'Oh, that,' said Randy with a dismissive wave. 'But I lost it even before I got a chance to use it.' He swallowed hard. 'I apologize for what I did. I'm sorry. But I need your help now. You have to help me get out of here. I can't do it on my own. My torch died and I tried to walk without light, but it was impossible. I had no idea where I was going.'

Travis glared at him. 'Oh, so now you need us. Give me one good reason why we should help you.'

Greg moved closer. 'Stop arguing, please. There's no time for that now. You can settle your scores later, when we get out. We're still in danger. We'd better hurry or they'll get us.' He turned to Kevin. 'You know where we are. So show us which way to go, how to reach the exit.'

Kevin didn't move. 'There are five of us now and we've all got guns.' A flash of anger darkened his eyes. Greg could see the muscles around his jaw tighten. 'Why don't we go back and make those bloodthirsty bastards pay for what they've done instead of running away?'

'I'm tired. All I want now is to get out of here and fly back home,' said Randy.

Chiara and Travis remained silent.

Greg cleared his throat. 'It wouldn't be a smart move, Kevin. They have more weapons than us, and probably know the underground much better than we do. Come on, let's go. We've wasted enough time. We don't know how long the light will last.'

They set off and, trying to make as little sound as possible, made their way through the maze of tunnels and caves that separated them from the exit. Kevin was walking ahead, keeping the torch beam far out in front of him. Chiara followed him closely, then Travis and Randy and finally, two steps behind, Greg. Although he willed his legs to move faster, they refused to obey. The adrenaline rush was ebbing away and he felt fatigue setting in.

'How far is it?' he asked in a hoarse voice.

'We're almost there. Don't you recognize where we are?'

He looked around. Countless black crystal particles embedded in the grey rock of the tunnel walls sparkled in the torchlight. Steep stairs rose ahead of them. Yes, he knew where they were. The exit from the underground was only a short distance away.

'We've made it. We escaped!' He breathed a

sigh of relief as he mounted the steps and entered the final tunnel that separated them from the outside world.

'Well, not quite. We shouldn't rush out. They could be lying in wait for us on the other side,' whispered Chiara.

Kevin nodded. 'You're right. We'd better be extra careful. One of us should check to see if the exit is clear, and if no one is—'

A hollow thud resounded, followed closely by a deafening rumble. The ground they were standing on shook. Dust filled the air. A few chunks of rock fell from the ceiling, one of them narrowly missing Greg.

The walls shuddered. Stones and rubble tumbled out, clattering to the floor. Panicked, they all hurried down the stairs.

'What was that, an earthquake?' Randy had a stunned look on his face.

'It sounded like a dynamite blast to me. The end of the tunnel must have collapsed,' said Travis.

'Yeah,' agreed Kevin. 'They must have got there before us and set off explosives to block the exit.'

'How did they manage that?'

'Manage what?'

'To get out before us?'

'I guess they know a shorter route.'

'We're lucky we're not hurt.' Chiara wiped away some of the dust coating her face.

'Yeah, but we're still trapped in this infernal place with no way out. You call that lucky?!' muttered Randy, his breath coming in quick, shallow gasps.

'Maybe the exit isn't completely blocked. We should check. Maybe we'll be able to clear a small passage and—'

'And fall into their hands? I'm sure they'll be out there waiting for us.'

'So what do we do now?' asked Greg.

Travis rubbed his chin. 'There has to be another exit.'

'That's the only one we know about,' said Kevin.

Chiara, who was pacing the floor of the small cave, stopped abruptly. 'The cenote,' she muttered, as if to herself.

'What?'

'The cenote,' she repeated, her voice rising an octave.

Randy stared at her, a look of blank incomprehension on his face. 'What about it?'

'We can try to get out through it.'

'I don't see how.'

'We'll climb up the wall to the top.'

'Climb up the wall? Oh, yeah, easy. It's at least twenty metres high. So tell me how, how are we going to climb it without any climbing gear?' he asked.

'Have you got a better idea?'

'No, but—'

'We have ropes,' interrupted Greg. 'Juan left a couple of ropes and some other tools in a cave he was working in a few days ago. I saw them lying on the floor. It's not far from here, I'll show you. If we tie them to some protruding tree roots, we could climb out of the cenote.'

'Well, I'm not so sure it will work, but I think it's worth a try,' agreed Travis. 'We don't have any other options.'

CHAPTER 19

After what seemed like an eternity, Travis reached the skylight opening at the top of the cenote. Tapping into the last reserves of his energy, he hauled himself over the rim and, with a stifled shout of triumph, landed on solid ground. He lay still, breathing so hard his sides burnt, the heady smell of damp soil and rotting vegetation filling his nostrils.

The rainforest erupted into a frenzy of sounds: the chirping of cicadas, the frog-like croaking of toucans, the vigorous calls of howler monkeys and the squawking of parrots. Branches swayed and leaves shook as dark shadows moved swiftly in the canopy of trees. He found all this bustling rather comforting after the emptiness and deathly silence of the underground.

He raised his head and let the cooling breeze play on his skin. The climb had worn him out. It was much tougher and more dangerous than he had imagined it would be. There were a few occasions when he'd feared he would lose his grip, plummet to the circular pool below and, not having enough strength to get out, drown. The turquoise blue waters scintillating in the pale light pouring through the opening in the cave roof looked so cool and tranquil, almost beckoning. But he suspected that beneath the calm surface it was treacherously deep and icy cold.

Besides, he knew what the ancient Maya used cenotes for. Human sacrifices. To please their rain god Chaac, they often threw children into them. The very idea of swimming in a pool of water where probably hundreds of skeletons lay, sent shivers down his spine.

He couldn't afford to rest for much longer. There was a good chance the thugs roamed the area. He had to help the others to reach the top and move somewhere safe. They risked being discovered if they lingered too long in one place.

He scrambled to his feet. The sky above, a startling combination of pale blue and pink shades, announced a new day. It made him realize that he had spent much more time in the vast maze of tunnels and caves beneath than he initially imagined he had. He moved with renewed urgency.

Several tall and sturdy trees surrounded the

rim of the cenote. He chose a robust ceiba tree that was perfectly positioned to serve his purpose, tied one end of the rope to its straight trunk and let the other end drop down the side of a cliff wall. Peering over the edge, he saw that Chiara had managed to grab hold of it.

Once Chiara had climbed up, Kevin got hold of the rope and followed her. Next, it was Randy's turn. Because of the injuries he had sustained from the fall in the red temple, he wasn't able to climb on his own, and they had to pull him out of the sinkhole. Finally, Greg climbed up to safety.

Once they'd all reached the top, Travis untied the rope.

'What are you going to do with that?' asked Greg.

'Leave it here. What else would I do with it?'

'Throw it into the water.'

'Why?'

'We shouldn't leave any trace of our presence here.'

'You have a point there,' Travis agreed.

'Which way now?' Randy stared through narrowed eyes at the tangled and mist-shrouded forest surrounding them on all sides.

Chiara glanced around. 'Let me see, we went that way. Then the tunnel turned … the small chamber … the stairs … the upper tunnel leading to the exit … Well, the camp must be over there somewhere.' She pointed to her left.

Travis frowned. 'The camp? I'm not sure it's safe to go to the camp.'

'Why? There's little chance the thugs are hanging around there. Why would they? They won't expect us to ever get out of the underground.'

'And what if you're wrong? We'd better be careful, just in case.'

'I need clothes. I can't walk around like this, can I?' Kevin tapped his bare chest, which was still smeared with blue paint.

Chiara folded her arms. 'More importantly, I'm hungry. It's been ages since we ate.'

Greg nodded. 'Yeah, we need food and water before we push on.'

'Sure we do. We won't be able to make it out of the jungle without sustenance. At least, I won't. I feel drained. So that's decided, we'll head for the camp. Lead the way!' Randy turned towards Travis, his green eyes burning into him.

'Why me?'

'Well, you're the jungle guide, right?'

Travis couldn't argue with that. His senses on high alert, he weaved his way through the undergrowth, pausing from time to time to get his bearings. The ground was soft and spongy, covered with a thick layer of dead leaves and branches that were made slippery by the morning dew. The dense tree canopy blocked much of the pale sunlight. As a result, the forest beneath was a dark tangled maze of vegetation, so dark that he could barely see where he was putting his feet.

'Are you sure we're heading in the right direction? We should have reached it by now,' said Chiara after they had been wandering for quite some time.

Travis stopped. She was right, they should be there by now. He looked into the murky gloom around them. His surroundings didn't look familiar at all. He ran a hand through his hair, feeling confused.

'It must be somewhere around here.' He was trying to convince himself as much as the others.

Greg shook his head. 'We're nowhere near. There are no temple mounds, and the vegetation looks different.'

'So, we're lost,' muttered Randy.

Kevin swatted at a mosquito that had landed on his arm, cursing under his breath. 'I need clothes. These bloodsuckers are eating me alive.'

Travis's backpack was digging into his shoulder, so he adjusted the strap. 'No, we're not lost. Trust me, the camp isn't far."

Greg wasn't convinced. 'I'm not sure we're headed in the right direction.'

'We have to keep on looking,' said Travis and moved deeper into the thicket, brushing aside vines and branches blocking his path.

They wandered around, searching, but they couldn't find the camp. Finally, Travis was forced to admit that he had lost all sense of direction and didn't know where they were.

'So, tell me how you're going to get us out of the jungle if you have no idea where we are.' Randy stared at him with a mixture of distrust and irritation.

Chiara shifted from one foot to the other. 'It will get lighter soon. It will be easier to find the way then.'

'So maybe we should wait,' suggested Kevin.

'No, it's best to keep moving. The camp must be somewhere around here. I'm sure we'll find it if we look a little further.'

They broadened their search area, then changed direction. Gradually, the fog thinned, and only smoky wisps trailed here and there. More and more sunshine filtered through the tree canopy above, creating dappled pools of silver light on the forest floor.

Chiara was right: it was easier to walk now.

Travis pushed aside some long, twisted liana stems dangling like thick ropes from a high branch.

'Wait!' Greg's voice stopped him in his tracks.

He turned towards him. 'Why? What's wrong?'

'There's something there.' Greg pointed. 'It looks like one of the temple mounds by the entrance to the dig site.'

'Where? I can't see anything.'

'Over there, between those two trees. You see it now?'

'Yeah … I can see something, but I can't

make out what it is.'

Travis pulled out his binoculars. 'You're right.' He peered through the lenses. 'Looks like we've finally found what we were looking for.' He wiped sweat from his brow and adjusted the focus. 'I can't see anyone around …' He scanned the rest of the area. '… but that doesn't mean it's safe.' He lowered his binoculars so they hung from the strap around his neck. 'They might be hiding somewhere in the bushes. We'd better be careful.'

They headed towards the camp, pushing their way through the dense vegetation. The trees thinned out, and a clearing appeared up ahead. Travis tiptoed closer, then ducked behind a bush and peered through the leaves.

'There's no one there.'

'Where are the tents?' asked Greg in a hushed voice, crouching beside him.

'That's exactly what I was asking myself,' he muttered, and raised the binoculars to his eyes. He could see the beaten down ground, footprints and imprints of tents in flattened grass.

'Those bloodthirsty bastards have taken them. They've cleared out all our stuff!' Chiara breathed close to Travis's ear. 'What are we going to do now?'

'Nice! We've got nothing to eat, nothing to drink, no clothes,' muttered Greg.

Travis lowered his binoculars. 'There's nothing we can do about it now. We'd better get going.'

Kevin leaned closer. 'At least we know where we are and which way to go now.'

'Yeah, but that doesn't help much. Without food and water we won't get far. Not in this heat. And it's getting hotter by the minute.' Randy's voice was hoarse, his face grim.

'We have to try. We don't have a choice, do we?'

'No. Not that I can think of.'

'So come on. Let's go.'

Randy pointed to a gnarly tree behind his back. 'The path must be there somewhere...'

'No. No path,' objected Greg, gesticulating to emphasize his words. 'We'll be too exposed. If the thugs are around somewhere, they'll see us. We should move through the thicket. It will be easier to hide in the underbrush.'

'Yeah, you're right. That's what we are going to do,' agreed Travis.

As they pushed on, the forest continued to thicken. They walked in silence, trying not to snap twigs or shake saplings. Travis paused every so often, listening intently if there was even the hint of a suspicious sound, and scanning the surrounding thicket for any sign of movement. All he saw were monkeys clambering among the trees, birds hopping from branch to branch. But no people. He started to relax.

They'd been trudging for almost an hour when he spotted a lighter area behind the tall and straight trunk of a mahogany tree. It looked like an illegal airstrip. Maybe it was the one he and Randy had seen before.

'What's wrong?' asked Chiara, when she saw him stop.

'Nothing's wrong. I think there's a clearing over there.' He pointed towards the lighter area. 'Don't move. None of you. Wait here. I'll go and check it out.'

Cautiously, he edged closer, glancing warily around. Then, hidden by a dense bush at the edge of the thicket, he looked through the binoculars. As far as the eye could see, a sun-beaten grassland stretched in front of him. He adjusted the focus and slowly scanned the area. He saw a fence made of wooden stakes and barbed wire, cattle grazing and what looked like a couple of rough-timbered shacks at the far end.

He went back.

'What is it? What did you see?' asked Randy.

'Just grassland.'

'Empty?'

'There's plenty of cattle grazing and I saw what looked like wooden cabins.'

'A cattle ranch? Does someone live there?'

'I don't know. I didn't see anyone.'

'Then we should go and check.' Kevin said. 'What are we waiting for? Come on. My throat is parched, I'm so thirsty. I need to get some water.'

'But it might not be safe. We don't know what or who we might stumble on.'

'Hey, don't be so afraid. We can defend ourselves if the need arises.' Kevin waved his weapon in the air. 'Come on,' he urged again.

As soon as they emerged onto the large and level pasture, Travis spotted a faint path meandering between coarse tufts of grass.

Squinting against the harsh sunshine, he pointed towards it. 'It probably leads to those wooden cabins.' He tilted his head to get a better view but couldn't see far enough to tell for sure.

They loaded their guns and made their way down the narrow trail. The grasses growing on both sides of it were so tall that they hid them almost completely from view. But there were no trees to provide shade and the sweltering sun was beating mercilessly down on their heads. The air was still and heavy. Not even the slightest breeze stirred the long blades of grass.

Travis's shirt was sticky with sweat. Beads of perspiration trickled down his face. With all his attention focused on the path ahead, he didn't even bother to wipe them away.

They were about fifty metres from the first wooden shack when its rickety door opened and a tough-looking, rather short man appeared in the doorway. Travis stopped and, shielding his eyes against the bright sun, tried to make out his features. But all he could see was that the stranger was wearing a white hat, its large brim obscuring his face.

The man took another step and froze. A gun

glinted in his right hand. He turned and called out to someone inside the hut. It was then that Travis managed to catch a glimpse of his face. He felt a prickle of unease stir the hairs at the nape of his neck. He recognized the man. He was one of the thugs he had seen in the underground! The others were probably inside the wooden shack.

His heart was pounding wildly in his chest. All he could think to do was run and look for cover. But in his stunned state, he was unable to move.

CHAPTER 20

'Run! It's them,' Travis finally managed to utter, his voice ringing with panic. 'Quick! Take cover!'

They stood rooted to the spot.

'Where? There's nowhere to—' mumbled Randy.

'Run! Hide! Anywhere. There!' He pointed to where the tall grass was growing along the fence, then crouching low, dashed for it himself.

The urgency in his voice and movements jolted the others into action. They followed his example. Just as they plunged into the grass, a succession of gunshots pierced the still air. Heavy footsteps pounded the ground.

Travis hid behind a waist-high clump of grass and peeked through it. The thugs were running their way, shooting. There were six of them, each one armed to the teeth.

He drew his weapon and fired a few warning shots. The thugs slowed down and ducked for cover.

In the silence that followed, he could hear blood roaring in his temples. The gun felt slick in his sweaty hand. He tightened his grip and turned towards his companions. 'We're too exposed here. We should hide in the forest.'

'Yeah, but do we get there? They'll kill us if we run out into the open,' hissed Greg.

He was right. To reach the thicket, they had to cross a large stretch of open plain. With almost nothing to hide behind, they would be an easy target. But what choice did they have?

'Use the cattle as cover,' suggested Chiara.

'Cattle? What do you mean?'

'Cross the fence. Hide behind the cattle. They won't dare to shoot and risk hurting the animals.'

Randy wasn't convinced. 'I'm not—'

'Yeah, that might work. It's worth a try,' interrupted Kevin, as he fired another warning shot.

Travis reloaded his gun. 'So come on, run. Go as far as you can. Now!'

'And you?'

'I'll stay to keep them at bay.'

Chiara remained where she was.

'Go!' he shouted.

'I'll stay here, with you.'

'No. Run!'

She didn't move.

Randy, Greg and Kevin reached the fence. They prised the barbed wire apart, and one by one, squeezed through the gap that appeared. Then, crouching low, they rushed across the pasture towards a herd of cows.

Travis and Chiara both fired a few rounds to scare off the thugs. They fired back, but didn't come any closer.

Travis glanced over his shoulder. 'It's okay now. Go! Run.'

'Be careful. Don't let them get you.' She scrambled to her feet.

'Don't worry, I won't. Now go!'

Chiara squeezed between the barbed-wire strands, and ran in the direction the others had gone.

Shifting his attention back to his enemies, Travis peered between the grass stalks. The rogues were creeping towards his hiding place. He had to stop them. No more warning shots this time, he had to hurt or kill someone. He took careful aim at the nearest brute, and pulled the trigger. A scream of pain split the air, and a crimson stain appeared above the man's left knee. He retreated, clutching his injured leg. The others fell to the ground and crawled back.

Deciding it was safe to leave his hiding place, Travis crossed the fence and rushed across the uneven pasture towards the grazing cattle. Shots resounded. A bullet whizzed past his head. He crouched lower to avoid being hit.

Halfway there, he tripped over a clump of grass and landed on his chest. Sore and flustered, he picked himself up and threw a quick glance behind. The thugs were crossing the barbed-wire fence. There was no time to lose. He gathered all his strength and quickened his pace.

A stray bullet grazed his left arm, and a searing pain erupted just above his elbow. Blood stained the fabric of his shirt, spreading in a bright red circle around the wound. He clenched his teeth, but didn't slow down. He spotted Chiara and Greg. A bit further, Randy and Kevin. They were scuttling among the cattle.

'The forest isn't far now,' he said when he'd caught up with them. 'We'll make it if we hurry up.'

Out of the corner of his eye, he caught movement. The thugs were getting closer faster than he'd expected. With a renewed sense of urgency, he lurched across the grassland, dodging behind the grazing animals.

Two gunshots cracked in the stifling air. He turned and saw, much to his surprise, that Randy and Kevin were the ones who'd fired them.

They shouldn't have done that, he thought. *A stupid move.*

More shots followed, and a nervous movement ran through the cattle. The ground shook as the panic-stricken animals charged in all directions. The noise was deafening. Travis had to sprint to and fro to keep clear of the scattering herd. A cloud of dust rose high into the air, obscuring his sight. When it diminished a little, he saw the others. To his relief, they seemed to be fine.

'We'd better stick together now,' said Chiara as he came closer.

They headed for the forest, running as fast as they could. Travis fired a few more rounds at the pursuers, then plunged into the dense undergrowth.

The lush vegetation enveloped him in a protective embrace. He heaved a sigh of relief. He waited for the others to join him, then pushed his way deeper into the jungle, cursing internally at the thorny branches scratching his skin and tearing at his clothes.

The further they went, the darker the forest became, as less sunshine was able to penetrate the dense canopy above. The hot air grew heavy, the humidity so thick that it felt like walking in a steam bath. There wasn't even a wisp of a breeze to offer any relief. Thirst more than hunger assailed Travis. He struggled to maintain a steady pace, and knew he wouldn't be able to keep it up for much longer. He looked over his shoulder. The others trailed several steps behind. He slowed down to let them catch up.

'I think we've lost them,' said Greg between gasps for breath.

'It's too early to be sure. They could be nearby.'

Kevin nodded. 'Yeah, we'd better be careful. I bet they won't give up easily. I'm sure they'll try to track us down.'

'So we mustn't slow down.'

'Yeah, we need to keep going.'

'I'm tired, I need some rest. I won't be able to keep up the pace much longer,' complained Randy.

Ignoring Randy, Chiara pointed to the wound on Travis's arm. 'You've been hurt?'

'Yeah, a bullet grazed my arm. It's nothing serious.'

'Let me see. It could be more serious than you think.'

'We can't afford to waste time now. It's okay, it's already stopped bleeding.'

They continued to push their way through the underbrush, Travis in the lead, gun drawn. Thick layers of moss and dead leaves absorbed the sound of their footfalls.

A sudden movement in the tangle of vegetation made him stop short. Something flashed through the trees. Was it an animal foraging in the underbrush, or was it the thugs? He raised his weapon and held his breath, listening, ears tuned to pick up the slightest sound, eyes straining to pierce the gloom. It was quiet, and then there was the sound of leaves rustling, twigs snapping. Then, once again, silence.

'What's that?' asked Kevin, alarmed.

Travis gestured for him to be silent and crouch low.

Making as little noise as possible, he ducked behind the nearest tree trunk and peered through a curtain of drooping vines. A dark shadow passed swiftly between the trees. Then another. Despite the feeble light, he recognized the brutes easily. They were trying to encircle them. Before he'd had time to warn the others, multiple cracks of gunfire resounded. He responded, firing into the trees.

More gunshots followed, and Greg, Chiara and Kevin returned the fire.

'We can't let them catch us.' Travis said and scurried into a clump of bushes.

'No way! They won't get us,' exclaimed Kevin, as he scampered over to him. Crouching down, he took careful aim and pulled the trigger. Nothing happened. He tried again. Still nothing. He shook the weapon angrily. 'Useless thing. It's empty.' He threw it to the ground. 'What now? I've got no gun.'

'Run! Just run and hide! That's what we must all do.'

Travis darted among the vegetation and, ducking behind trees and bushes, fired at the enemy he couldn't see. He kept running as fast as he could, throwing glances over his shoulder every now and then to make sure the others were following. He was so focused on getting away that he didn't think about which way he was going.

His lungs were beginning to burn with the need for air. He slowed down to catch his breath. He listened, but couldn't hear any sounds of pursuit. The jungle was quiet. Unusually quiet. Even the birds and monkeys were silent, and the cicadas had stopped droning. He couldn't even hear a mosquito buzzing. Unease prickled his skin. It felt like the calm before the storm.

The others caught up with him.

'I'm exhausted. We need to find a safe place to hide and take a rest,' muttered Randy.

'Yeah, but there's nothing here.' Greg glanced around.

Travis pushed aside several thick and twisted liana stems that were blocking his way. 'So we'll have to keep on moving until we find somewhere suitable.'

'And what if we don't? I'm so tired, I really need to have a rest.'

He shrugged. 'We all do. Hold on a little longer.'

'Come on. We shouldn't linger too long in one spot,' urged Kevin.

'We'd better keep quiet. They might hear us,' cautioned Chiara.

They continued trudging through the lush jungle in silence. Suddenly, Travis caught the sound of a movement somewhere nearby. He spun, aiming his gun in the direction it was coming from.

'It's them, they've found us.' Randy fumbled for his weapon.

A dark shadow darted from tree to tree, moving with swift agility and, in an instant, disappeared among the foliage. Travis lowered his pistol. 'No need to panic. It was only a spider monkey. Come on.'

Gesturing for the others to follow him, he took a few more steps forward. Another movement caught his eye. A figure rose from a bush, rifle glinting.

Gunfire exploded.

He jumped under a bush just in time to avoid being hit. He flattened himself against the grass and dead leaves, and lay still for a while, the cloying smell of damp earth and rotting vegetation filling his nostrils. He let a few more seconds pass before he dared to peek through the foliage.

The thug ducked behind a tree, then reappeared, gun cocked.

Travis took careful aim and pulled the trigger. The man's back arched, his head cranked skyward and he toppled to the jungle floor without making a sound.

Travis stifled a cry of triumph. One thug down!

More shots came, reminding him that the fight wasn't over yet.

He heard a sudden cry of pain and saw Chiara slump to the ground. Acting on instinct, he slithered through the foliage towards her. 'Were you hit? Where? Let me see.'

She whimpered and, eyes rolling, nodded at her thigh. Blood seeped through the fabric of her trousers, pooling around her leg. She pressed her hand into the wound, trying to staunch the bleeding, but blood oozed between her fingers, staining them crimson.

Travis tore her trouser leg open. He pulled a clean shirt out of his backpack and ripped it into strips which he knotted together and tied around the wound to stop the flow of blood. Then, with Kevin's aid, he hauled Chiara deeper into the bushes, out of sight of the attackers.

The gunshots stopped. The buzzing of mosquitoes seemed unnaturally loud in the suddenly silent forest. He waited some more but all was quiet.

Travis turned towards Kevin. 'Stay here with Chiara. I'll go and see what's going on.'

He had barely crawled out of the hiding place when he heard the sound of footsteps crunching on dead leaves. He froze, finger curled around the trigger, eyes fixed on the direction from which the noise had come. A second later, thick lianas hanging from a giant ceiba tree moved and the figure of a man emerged.

It was Greg.

'Why is it so quiet? Are all the thugs dead?'

Travis lowered the gun.

'I wish they were, but no such luck. Two of the brutes fled.' He ran a hand over his face. 'I kept firing but they managed to dodge the bullets.'

'So the fight isn't over yet. What about Randy? Where is he?'

'I … I don't know. I was too busy shooting to watch him.'

Travis cupped his hands around his mouth and called, 'Randy!'

There was no answer.

'We must find him. You search this part.' He pointed to his left. 'And I'll go over there.'

He had only taken a couple of steps when he saw a man lying on his back, arms and legs splayed, his chest a bloody mess. It was one of the thugs. A bit further on, he stumbled upon another dead body. Another thug. He kept searching, looking behind each bush and tree. Randy was nowhere to be seen.

He took another step forward, pushing gigantic fern fronds out of his way when he heard Greg call, 'Here, I've found him.'

He hurried over to him. Randy lay slumped against a tree trunk, clutching his right shoulder. Blood oozed through his fingers.

'I got hit. Can't stop the bleeding,' he moaned through clenched teeth.

Travis crouched down beside him. 'Let me see it.'

It looked as though the bullet had only grazed his right shoulder. But it had torn out quite a chunk of flesh with it. So although the wound wasn't deep, it was bleeding a lot.

With a few strips of cloth torn from his shirt, Travis made a makeshift dressing. When he offered to help him stand up, Randy waved him off. 'It's fine, I'll manage.'

They went back to where they'd left Chiara and Kevin. The wound on Chiara's thigh was still bleeding. It was more serious than he'd first thought. The makeshift dressing wasn't enough. She needed urgent medical attention. But the civilized world was so far away.

Travis took a few more clean strips of fabric and wrapped them around the wound. There wasn't much else he could do. 'You think you'll be able to stand up?' he asked.

'I don't know. It hurts like hell … give me a hand.' She winced in pain as he and Greg helped her to her feet. She leaned on him heavily. 'It won't be easy to walk, but we have to get out of here, so I've got no choice but to try.'

'It'll be days before we get out of the jungle … if we ever do,' muttered Kevin. 'I'm tired and so thirsty I could drink a lake dry.'

'We'd better move on while we've still got the strength. Which way should we go?' asked Greg.

Travis pointed to his left.

They set off, plodding through the thicket, step after slow step. To spare their energy, they took it in turns helping Chiara.

The sun rose higher in the sky. More and more daylight filtered through the canopy above, casting dappled patterns on the forest floor. The visibility improved but the uneven ground and the dense vegetation made it difficult to walk, and the stifling heat and high humidity were sapping their energy so that, although they tried, they couldn't move any faster.

Travis felt Chiara sag against his shoulder. She was shivering as if she were cold and her breathing was ragged. A spray of hair was plastered to her forehead. Beads of sweat rolled down the sides of her face. Her pallid cheeks had taken on a waxy sheen, and her eyes were bleary, dulled with pain. He wasn't sure she was going to make it out of the jungle alive.

CHAPTER 21

Despite the sultry heat of the jungle sapping their energy, they plodded on with dogged determination. Mosquitoes, smelling human sweat and blood, went into a frenzy and attacked them in swarms. Their constant buzzing and itchy bites were maddening. Swatting them didn't help, it only made those irritating bloodsuckers more aggressive.

Step by weary step, Travis weaved his way through the tangled mass of vegetation, struggling to keep his senses alert for danger. His throat and stomach burned, begging for water and food. For a time, he ignored their pleas as best he could, but they only became more and more insistent and he knew he wouldn't be able to go on for much longer.

'You think those two thugs who escaped will try to track us down?' asked Kevin.

He shrugged. 'I don't know. Maybe.'

A dark shape loomed ahead. Travis couldn't make out any details yet but thought it looked strangely familiar. As he drew nearer, he realized it was one of the two huge human stone heads he and Randy had seen earlier on their way to the dig site. It proved they were heading in the right direction, but at the same time told him they had still a long way to go. His shoulders sagged with disappointment. It seemed as if they had been walking for hours, and yet they hadn't gone that far. At this rate, it would take them days to reach civilization.

'What the heck is that?' exclaimed Greg. 'A head. A huge stone head! What a find, it's splendid.' He moved closer.

'Come on. There's no time to admire it now,' said Randy. 'If we stop at every piece of stonework we come across, we'll never make it out of here.'

'I'm so thirsty,' muttered Chiara, sagging against Kevin's shoulder. 'Water. I need some water. It's so hot. I can't stand the heat. And my thigh … the wound … it burns … it hurts like hell.'

Travis looked at her. She looked exhausted, on the brink of collapse.

'Hold on just a little bit longer. I'm sure we'll find some water soon.' Kevin tried to reassure her.

Empty promises, thought Travis. He knew there was no water around here.

Greg leaned against the cold stone of the ancient structure. 'Why don't we take a short break? I'm dog tired. I can hardly move. Every muscle in my body is crying out for rest.'

Travis nodded. 'Yeah, not a bad idea. It will do us good. We are all tired.' He shrugged off his backpack and reloaded his gun.

A flicker of surprise crossed Greg's face. 'You think you'll need to use it soon? That the thugs will find us?'

'Use what? The gun?'

Greg nodded.

'I don't know, but I don't want to be caught unprepared. In this part of the jungle danger is never far away.' Travis straightened up. 'Well, I have to go now. I need to check something. You stay here and take care of Chiara.'

'Go where? Alone? What if the thugs attack us?'

'Don't worry, I won't be long.'

'Wait! Where are you going?'

'There's an airstrip nearby.'

'An airstrip? And you think you'll find a plane standing there, just waiting for us, ready to take off? You wish! There'll be nothing,' said Greg. 'Don't waste your time and energy. It would be better to stay here and take a rest.'

'Yeah,' agreed Randy. 'You're just wasting

your time.'

Kevin scratched his head. 'A plane could get us out of this green hell in about an hour. So it's probably worth checking.'

Greg shrugged. 'Okay. Suppose we find a plane. Then what? Who is going to fly it?'

Kevin wasn't so easily discouraged. 'I could try. I've done it before.'

Travis swatted at a mosquito buzzing around his ear. 'I'm going now. Just stay where you are. Be patient, wait until I get back.'

Pushing aside the tangled vegetation, he headed in the direction of the airstrip. He realized that the chances of finding a plane were slim, but he was unable to resist the urge to check, just in case.

It was more difficult than he thought to find his way back to the clearing. It took him over ten minutes to get there. Making as little noise as possible, he tiptoed to its edge. Then, hidden behind a gnarly tree trunk, he peered through a mass of branches and leaves. He blinked, hardly believing his eyes. At the far end of the long grassy runway stood a small plane, sunlight glinting off its sleek white fuselage and wings.

His heart began to beat faster. He tilted his head to get a better view. It looked big enough to accommodate all of them. As he kept staring, he detected a slight motion. So subtle that it was barely perceptible. Yet it was there.

Panic seized him. Was the plane about to take

off? His first impulse was to run out into the clearing and ask for help, but he resisted, deciding it would be too risky. His gut instinct told him he'd better check who was inside first. He clung tighter to the tree and squinted through the binoculars at the cockpit.

Relief smoothed the furrow between his brows when he saw that the cockpit was empty. It must have been the distorted hot air that created the illusion of movement.

Slowly, he scanned the rest of the aircraft and the surrounding area. There was no one to be seen anywhere. He felt a surge of excitement. Full of fresh hope, he smiled. Like Kevin had said, a plane would get them out of the jungle in about an hour. It meant they could get Chiara the medical attention she needed. She could be saved. Adrenaline coursed through his body. He hurried back to the others.

'And? Nothing, just as I told you?' asked Greg as soon as he saw him.

Travis shook his head. 'There's a plane. Empty, ready to board.'

'Really? I don't believe you!'

'I'm serious, but we'd better hurry or our luck may run out.'

They set off immediately. Travis led the way, followed by Greg and Kevin who supported Chiara. Then, finally, Randy. Despite being wounded and tired, they maintained a steady pace and stopped only when they reached the edge of the clearing.

Taut with nervous anticipation, Travis peered through the foliage separating him from the grassy runway. The plane was still there, standing in exactly the same place as before.

He raised his binoculars to get a closer look.

'It looks empty. I can't see anyone. Let's go!' He pushed aside the low-hanging branches and was about to step out onto the makeshift airstrip when the bushes on the other side of the forest quivered. Two men emerged, one of them limping.

He ducked behind a tree trunk, pulling Chiara and Kevin with him, just in time to avoid being seen and, once again, looked through the binoculars. 'It's them,' he whispered, his eyes flicking from one man to the other.

'You mean the two thugs who managed to escape?' asked Greg.

He nodded.

Greg's knuckles whitened as he tightened his grip on the gun's handle. 'This time we mustn't let them get away! Those bastards have to pay for what they've done.' He moved a step closer to the edge and fired twice at the two unsuspecting thugs. But he was too nervous to take a proper aim, and he missed.

Instantly, the two rogues lay down on the ground and began to crawl towards the plane. Travis realized he had to act fast if he wanted to stop them. The gun jerked as he pulled the trigger. He too, missed. Cursing his own ineptness, he fired once more. A split second too late. The thugs had already taken cover behind the fuselage. Again, he missed.

He glanced over his shoulder at Kevin. 'Take Chiara and move deeper into the forest. Hide somewhere safe. Do it. Now!'

'No,' protested Chiara, fumbling for her weapon. 'It's my leg that is injured, not my hands. I can still be useful. I can shoot.'

'But you can't run.'

'I can crawl.'

He could see there was no use arguing, her mind was made up.

More gunfire cracked through the air. A hail of bullets peppered the surrounding forest. Bark splintered. Twigs snapped off. Shredded foliage showered the jungle floor just a couple of inches away from where they were squatting. They ducked deeper into the bushes.

Randy found cover behind a large fern growing on a fallen tree trunk, where he huddled and waited for the attack to stop. Crouching low, Kevin and Greg moved a few metres further on, trying to get a better aim at the two thugs. Chiara fell to the ground and crawled closer to the edge of the clearing. Travis stayed by her side, determined to protect her.

He reloaded his gun and fired a few more rounds at the two thugs creeping between the wheels, but they moved with such speed and agility that it was difficult to target them. They managed to dodge every bullet. His frustration mounted with each missed shot.

Backs flattened against the fuselage, the thugs edged their way towards the door of the plane, firing with relentless rage. The first one, a barrel-chested and round-faced man, probably the pilot, yanked the door open and sprang inside while the second thug, whom Travis recognized as the leader of the gang, kept shooting.

The pilot started the engine. The gang leader moved closer, ready to climb aboard.

They were going to flee! He had to stop them!

Gripping the gun so tightly that his knuckles whitened, Travis aimed it at the man's head and pulled the trigger. Nothing happened. No bullet came out. The magazine was empty. Frantic, he fumbled inside his backpack. There were no more bullets. He cursed under his breath, seething with helpless rage.

Chiara squeezed the trigger, and the sound of gunfire cut through the air. Blood spread across the thug's left shoulder. Halfway through the door, he swayed. But his legs held. In an instant he regained his balance and dashed inside. Chiara fired one more time. A split second too late. She missed. The bullet smashed into the wing, ripping off bits of metal. She swore and lowered her gun.

The door slammed shut.

The small white plane quivered, darted forward, skimmed along the ground, then rose into the air. Greg rushed out of the bushes, rage and despair twisting his features. He fired a few rounds at the aircraft as it flew away.

'Bastards! Once again they've managed to get away,' he snarled, waving his gun.

Travis helped Chiara to her feet. Anger washed over him like an ocean wave. His jaw clenched as he stared at the receding plane.

Randy emerged from the thicket. 'What now? We are left with nothing.'

'Yeah, nothing. No plane. So all we can do is walk.' Travis gasped, his eyes widening in disbelief. A ribbon of black smoke curled up from the machine cutting through the hazy blue sky. Within seconds, the ribbon had grown into a dense cloud. A shiver of excitement ran through him as he put the binoculars to his eyes.

The small plane nose-dived and crashed into the dense jungle below.

'Well done, Greg. You hit it!' He lowered the binoculars.

'Really? It went down? You sure?'

'Yes, I'm sure. I just saw it. So they didn't escape after all!'

'Unless they survived the crash.'

'Impossible!'

Kevin gave a yelp of joy. 'Finally, they've got what they deserved.'

Randy straightened up, impatience flickering in his eyes. 'Well, we'd better get going. We still have a long journey ahead of us.'

They re-entered the thicket and trudged deeper and deeper, the humidity draining their strength with unexpected speed. The forest darkened. Very little sunlight now penetrated the dense canopy above. A fog descended, swirling among the branches of the trees and hovering above the ground. It became harder and harder to find their way through the tangled mass of vegetation.

Travis tried to ignore all the inconveniences, focusing on the road ahead, but as the day wore on, his mood sank. The thirst and hunger became almost impossible to bear, forcing him to slow his stride to an almost snail's pace. He had lost track of time. He didn't know how long they had been walking, nor how far they had yet to go. He wasn't even sure they were heading in the right direction. The wound on his arm flared with a burning sensation. The skin around it had become swollen and inflamed.

With the back of his hand he wiped sweat off his forehead and licked his parched lips. What he needed most was water. He knew that without it he wouldn't be able to hold on much longer. And what then? The worst-case scenarios began playing through his mind, and he tried to shake them off.

It was now his turn to help Chiara walk, and he almost had to drag her as she hardly had any strength left. Her arm weighed more and more heavily on his shoulders. Her breathing was laboured and shallow, her skin pale and coated with sweat. Despite the heat, she shivered slightly. He glanced over his shoulder at the others. All three looked on the verge of collapse.

'Let's take a rest,' he suggested.

'Better not. As long as I keep moving, I'm fine. If I stop ... I'm not sure I'll be able to get going again,' said Greg between gasps for breath.

'My shoulder ... it hurts so much ... it burns. I think I need to change the dressing soon,' groaned Randy.

'Hold on a bit longer. We have to find a more suitable place.'

Travis saw a fallen tree blocking his passage. The stumpy trunk was almost entirely covered in moss with a couple of fresh green ferns sprouting in its middle. As he stepped around it, he caught a whiff of woodsmoke. He frowned, wondering whether his senses were deceiving him. He sniffed the air harder and this time he knew he hadn't imagined it. There it was, the faint but unmistakable odour of burning wood. He shook his head, a spark of hope kindling inside him. Woodsmoke meant fire. Fire meant people. People meant help.

Was there a village nearby?

Then, as soon as it had appeared, his optimism faded. The jungle was a dangerous place. You never knew what kind of people you would come across. *We'd better be careful until we find out who is out there*, he thought.

'What is it? Is something wrong?' Kevin's face was taut with alarm.

'I can smell woodsmoke,' he said, lowering his voice almost to a whisper, and motioned for him to take hold of Chiara. 'Wait here. I'll go and check where it's coming from. I need a gun.'

Without a word, Chiara handed him hers.

Travis traipsed through the underbrush, following the acrid scent of burning wood as it grew stronger. He slowed down and, advancing with a stealthy step, scanned the lush vegetation surrounding him on every side. All he could see were fleeting shadows accompanied by a soft rustle as some unidentified animals – disturbed by the unexpected intrusion of a human being – scurried away. Somewhere up in the canopy, a spider monkey emitted a long, high-pitched screech, alerting others to danger. A parrot squawked and flapped its wings.

He took a few more quiet steps, then, crouching low, hid in the underbrush and looked through the binoculars. He saw nothing at first, just a tangle of greenery. But then he could make out more detail, and he noticed a tiny clearing, with a smouldering fire in the middle of it. Silver-grey tufts of smoke – which he initially mistook for wisps of fog – were still rising from it.

He adjusted the focus to sharpen the vision, and once again scanned the area. Wedged between two stout palm trees flanking one side of the opening, stood a dingy shack, nothing more than a thatched palm-frond roof nestling on a crude, windowless wooden structure. There was no one in sight.

Step by cautious step he got nearer and peered into the hut. He saw two low-hanging hammocks, various-sized bags strapped to wooden poles, plastic buckets and canisters, a few pieces of clothing and some other items scattered around. He wondered whether the canisters contained water and the bags food. He stepped inside. With trembling fingers he began to unscrew the lid of a large container that was filled almost to the brim with clear liquid, hoping it was water, hoping to be finally able to quench his agonizing thirst. Just then, he heard branches being pushed aside.

Footsteps crunched through dead leaves and fallen twigs, releasing the odour of decay. Someone was coming.

It was too late to run away.

He drew his gun and turned around. Something white fluttered through the foliage. His finger curled around the trigger, ready to squeeze it. The bushes parted and a man emerged from the shadows. Right behind him, another. Thick ropes wrapped around their waists, the machetes and the milky, white sap of the sapodilla tree they carried told him they were *chicleros*. The kind of men he usually chose to avoid because, from what he had heard, they could be violent and dangerous.

The two men froze when they saw the gun

being pointed at them.

'Drop your weapons!' Travis ordered.

Neither of the men moved. They just kept staring at him, their dark, shiny eyes narrowed into slits, as if they were trying to guess his intent.

'I told you, drop your weapons or I'll shoot!' he repeated, his voice sounding far more threatening than he felt.

With a show of reluctance, they threw their machetes and revolvers to the ground. He kicked them aside.

'What do you want?' asked the shorter of the two, while Greg searched him to make sure he wasn't hiding any other weapons.

The other man kept silent. Then, suddenly, he lunged at Travis with astonishing speed and force. Pain exploded in his body. He staggered and lost his grip on the gun. The attacker grabbed him in a headlock. He writhed like a snake, kicked and clawed.

The man's clutch on his windpipe tightened. Frantic, Travis gasped for air. Suddenly, he felt the cold steel of a gun barrel digging into his abdomen.

'Stop fighting. You can't win. Don't move or I'll blow you away,' hissed the shorter man, who was holding the pistol. The ferocious gleam in his eyes told Travis that he meant what he said. He had no choice but to surrender.

'Listen, I mean no harm. All I want is to get out of the jungle as soon as possible. I'm lost and thirsty. I need water … I need your help,' he stammered between gasps for air.

'Oh, now you need help.' The corners of the rogue's mouth tugged up into a brief grin. He poked him harder with the gun. 'You have no business nosing around our camp. What were you looking for?' A flicker of distrust crossed his tanned, deeply lined and weather-beaten face.

'Water. I was looking for water … and something to eat.'

The man eyed him from head to toe. 'Are you alone?'

'No. There are four of us.'

'Four? So where are the others? Where are they hiding?' His wary gaze swept the surrounding thicket. 'Do they have guns?'

'One of them, a woman, is badly injured. She's got a large, open wound on her leg. She needs help, fast. Trust me, it's really serious, it's a matter of life and death. She's lost a lot of blood and is too weak to walk. She'll die if you won't help us. She needs to see a doctor.'

'A doctor? We are no doctors, man. There are no doctors anywhere around here.'

'All I ask for is water and food. Please, help us.'

The two *chicleros* exchanged silent glances.

The shorter man lowered his gun. 'Okay, show us where they are. Come on. Move! Take us to where they are hiding. But I warn you, don't try anything stupid. If I see anything suspicious,

J.A. KALIS

I'll kill you.'

266

CHAPTER 22

Six months later

A fine mist descended, wrapping a thin veil around every tree and shrub, giving the jungle a rather eerie and sinister appearance. Here and there, a few wisps, ragged and white like puffs of smoke, drifted among leafy branches and ropey lianas. Daylight faded into a murky gloom and, although it was only early afternoon, it felt more like evening. Shadows deepened and lengthened, creating the illusion of some giant creatures crouching behind tree trunks and primordial ferns.

Travis plodded on, with undiminished determination, deeper and deeper into the lush and steamy thicket. His attention focused ahead, he pushed through clusters of broad-leafed plants and weaved between huge trees draped with tenacious vines, his boots sinking into the spongy layer of decaying vegetation carpeting the ground and squelching on patches of sticky mud. The dense overhead canopy didn't allow even the slightest breeze to pass, so the air beneath was stiflingly hot and muggy, and heavy with the pungent smell of damp earth and rotting wood released with each step.

He swept a sleeve across his forehead, aware of the thick drops of sweat that had gathered on it like condensation on a windowpane, and adjusted the straps of his backpack so that they wouldn't dig into his shoulders. He stumbled on a protruding root and would have lost his footing if not for his sharp reflexes. Swearing, he flung out his arms and grabbed onto some thick vines hanging from a branch of a huge mahogany tree, saving him from a hard fall and giving enough support for him to regain his balance.

He took a few swigs of water to calm himself down and rehydrate. It was the first time in six months that he'd set foot in the jungle, the first time since their narrow escape from the underground caves. He still remembered every moment of the strenuous journey through the rainforest as vividly as if it were yesterday.

They had had a lot of luck that day to have stumbled upon the two *chicleros* who turned out to be more kind-hearted than their rough looks and manners suggested. They had given them food and water, and had helped them get to Flores safely. If it weren't for them, they would have all died in the jungle from thirst, infection or exhaustion.

After the necessary medical treatment, Randy had quickly recovered from his injuries and flown back home. However, Chiara's thigh wound was so severe that she'd had to stay in hospital for a couple of weeks. Travis had visited her a few times, but after she'd been discharged and gone home, they lost contact.

The sepulchral ruins buried deep under the jungle floor didn't remain forgotten. Another group of archaeologists and anthropologists were sent to scour the vast subterranean maze of gloomy caves and tunnels for remnants of the ancient civilization, trying to uncover its long-held secrets.

When Travis heard that the dig site had been reopened and that Kevin and Greg were among the new research team, he decided to go back. Despite the danger, the first quick visit ignited his curiosity. He was intrigued to find out more about it and take a closer look at the amazing sculptures, murals and enigmatic artefacts. He wondered whether Chiara had also returned to continue her work. He really hoped she had and that he would see her again.

To his dismay, the journey through the *Petén* lowlands took even longer this time than on the previous trip. Poor visibility due to bad weather made progress slow and difficult. Although he had set off at dawn, he still had a way to go before reaching the camp. If he continued at such a slow pace, he wasn't sure he would get there before full darkness settled. But he was too exhausted to quicken his step.

Hour after hour he struggled through the tangled mass of lush vegetation that clawed at his clothes and scratched his skin. Then, finally, he saw some moss and lichen-covered stones and earthen mounds entombing the ancient treasures. The trees thinned out and he emerged into the small clearing where the archaeologists had set up their camp. There were more tents now than last time. It looked like the present team was much bigger and better equipped than the previous one.

He spotted two men standing under a large tarp stretched over the kitchen area, and as he got closer, he saw that one of them was Kevin. He noticed they both carried guns.

Kevin greeted him with a nod. 'Perfect timing. The evening meal is almost ready.'

'Good, I'm starving.' He shrugged off his backpack. 'Gosh, I'm so exhausted, I can barely stand. Where is everybody? Down in the underground?'

'Yeah, still working. But they should be up soon.'

He put up a tent and waited. Dusk fell. The sky, visible through a break in the canopy, turned indigo blue. Countless stars studded it, twinkling. Kevin and the other man lit more torches to illuminate the whole camp.

About an hour later, Travis saw flickering light at the cave's mouth, and then several figures emerged. His heart pounding, he scanned their faces. He saw Greg, but no Chiara. He felt a stab of disappointment. But then two other men and a woman stepped out. His breath caught in his throat when he recognized Chiara's shapely silhouette. He noticed she still walked with a slight limp.

Chiara lifted her head and their gazes met. She stopped. Pale moonlight reflected off her face, her eyes glinting with an emotion he couldn't quite read.

'What a surprise to see you here! I had no idea you were a part of our team,' she said as she walked over to him.

'I'm not. I came back because I'm curious to find out more about this place.'

'So tell me …' Travis asked Chiara later, after they'd had supper and talked for a while. '… what are those caves? *Xibalba*, the Maya underworld? Vestiges of an ancient city? Or just a mystical place where strange, sinister rituals were practised? Why there, why so deep in the underground?'

'Well, to tell you the truth, we don't know for sure what this place is yet. It could be the Maya *Xibalba*, but it could also be all the other things you mentioned,' she replied. 'This underground network of tunnels and caverns is huge. Much bigger than we first thought, and we have examined only a small part of it so far. It's too early to draw conclusions. What we know for certain is that the Maya were obsessed with caves. Caves and cenotes were for them gateways to the underworld, sacred places where gods of creation and destruction lived.'

'And what about all the skeletons we've seen scattered around the subterranean chambers? Were all those people killed to appease the Maya gods? Were they victims of human sacrifices? If so, then what drove the Maya to make so many sacrificial offerings in those remote, dark places? The twisted minds of their spiritual leaders? Or maybe the threat of a disaster?'

'Yes, the remains belong to victims of human sacrifice from different time periods. But most of the bones date back to the ninth century, which coincides with the collapse of the Maya civilization. Judging by what we found, there was a burst of activity in the underground during that period. It seems as if by performing more rituals, the Maya were desperately trying to ward off a looming disaster.'

'What kind of disaster? What made the Maya abandon their prosperous cities and move elsewhere?'

'Water shortage. Which, I'd say, was partly their own doing. For centuries, it was common practice among the Maya to cut down and burn the forest to clear land for agricultural or construction plots. Isn't it asking for trouble? It surely is. They clearly didn't know what we know now about the benefits of forests, about the crucial role they play in climate regulation. Forests generate rainfall. Trees are rainmakers.' She paused, tucked a strand of hair behind her ear, then continued. 'The population grew fast, and more and more trees were logged. There's no doubt in my mind that the misguided deforestation contributed to the climate change which occurred at the end of the eighth and the beginning of the ninth century. Temperatures rose. Rainfall became sparse. Droughts plagued the lowlands. Severe droughts. Some of them lasted as long as eighteen years. Can you imagine, eighteen years without a drop of rain?' A fierce gleam brightened her eyes as she fixed them on his. 'The Maya depended on the rains to replenish their water supplies, so lack of rainfall for such an extended period of time had a devastating impact on their lives. Water reservoirs ran dry. The fertile soil of the heartland was parched. Crops died. There was not enough food to feed everyone. Famine forced people to flee the region. And so the once flourishing cities emptied out. Then once again, years after the destructive actions of people stopped, the rains returned and the jungle reclaimed its territory.'

'You mean the sacrificial offerings were

connected to the droughts?'

'Yes. No doubt whatsoever. Most of them were made to Chaac, the rain god who – according to the ancient Maya beliefs – dwelled in caves, gushing with subterranean rivers, and water-filled cenotes. You know what rain for the Maya was?'

He shook his head.

'The rain god's tears. They believed that when Chaac cried, rain fell on the Earth. And as rain played such an important role in their lives, they were ready to do anything to please Chaac. Chaac was a very important deity in the Mayan pantheon. Twice a year they performed rituals to worship him, offering food, various material goods and human blood. When severe droughts affected the heartland, they increased the number of rituals and human sacrifices. And the rituals became more violent. The victims were stripped, painted blue, then thrown on a stone altar where their hearts were ripped out, and still beating, offered to Chaac. Yes, the extremely resistant pigment known as the Maya blue, a unique vibrant azure colour – just like the sky on a clear day – was the colour of Chaac and of human sacrifice.'

'Oh, that's why the thugs in the cave painted your colleagues blue. But, despite the incessant pleas and numerous sacrifices, the rains didn't come.'

'No, not a drop fell from the sky. So they

ventured deeper and deeper into the gloomy underground, into the very realm of the rain god, pleading with him to bring relieving rains down on the Earth. Yet despite numerous prayers and offerings, the droughts persisted and instead of diminishing, intensified. It seemed that what they offered wasn't enough. That Chaac grew thirsty. Thirsty for blood. Driven by desperation, in an ultimate attempt to quench Chaac's excessive thirst, they offered children, especially young boys whom they considered pure and unspoiled.'

'But it didn't help, did it? Still no rain came.'

'No, it didn't help.'

'So what did they do? Stopped the rituals and fled?'

'Yes, many fled. But the interesting part is that the killings didn't stop altogether. We found proof they have continued until the present time. Although on a much smaller scale. It seems that year after year a small group of people return to the caves to perform rituals, making offers to the ancient gods.'

'Blood offers? Human sacrifices?'

She nodded.

'Just like those who attacked us?'

'Yeah.'

Before they went to their tents, Travis asked Chiara, 'How is work going?'

'Slow. Much slower than I'd expected. Some inscriptions are quite fragmentary. Due to discolouration and erosion, many of the glyphs are difficult to make out. It's hard to read them. Hard to fill in the gaps. It takes a lot of time and effort. I'm worried that I will misinterpret the texts or miss some valuable information that could shed more light on the ancient Maya life. After weeks of hard work, there's still lots to be done. What I've studied up to now is only a small fraction. This place is so huge. There must be many more inscriptions, still hidden, waiting to be discovered. But I'm too busy to search for them.'

'I could help.'

'Really? Are you sure?'

He nodded.

'I could definitely use your help. But you'll have to stay here for a few weeks.'

'No problem, I've got time to kill. And I'd be really happy to help.'

'And you know your way around the underground. That's a big advantage. I can hardly refuse such an offer, can I?'

'Great, I can start tomorrow.'

THIRST OF THE RAIN GOD

Thank you for reading **THIRST OF THE RAIN GOD**. I hope you enjoyed it!

Do You Want to Help the Author? You Can Make A Difference.

If you enjoyed reading this book, the best thing you can do to help is tell others about it and write an honest review. Even a sentence or two will help. You can create a review for **THIRST OF THE RAIN GOD** on Amazon, Goodreads and BookBub.

Thank you SO much.

You might also like my other novels:

WHEN THE JAGUAR SLEEPS

The Curse Of Inca Gold Book 1

ASIN: B0187T2R6U

Non-stop action. An enthralling treasure hunting adventure in the Amazon rainforest in Ecuador.

A dream holiday turns into a nightmare when two men are stranded in the Amazon rain forest after a plane crash. With no hope of being rescued, they decide that their only chance of survival is to find their way back to civilization. And so they set off on a daring journey, struggling through the dense underbrush, totally unprepared for the dangers that lie ahead. When they stumble upon some ancient ruins where fabulous treasures might be hidden, it all goes wrong again …

WRATH OF THE JAGUAR MAN

The Curse Of Inca Gold Book 2

ASIN: B07BS9GRKB

A high-octane thriller full of unexpected twists and turns that will take you on a roller coaster ride of mystery and edge-of-your-seat suspense into the heart of the Amazon jungle, to Paris and harsh, semi-arid plains of south western Spain.

THE TRAVEL MATE

ASIN: B01LK1XZ2C

A gritty, chilling, fast-paced thriller that will have you on the edge of your seat!. This story is about how a family makes a frenzied and terrifying journey searching for their loved one, a young woman, gone missing while trekking in a remote mountain region.

Made in the USA
Las Vegas, NV
19 April 2022

47695281R00166